HELL AND BACK

THE DEVIL'S DAUGHTER (BOOK 6)

G.A. CHASE

BAYOU MOON PRESS, LLC

ABOUT THIS BOOK

Time is quickly running out for Sere to save the world. Marjory Laroque has all that she needs to create her immortal army. Even worse, Aloysius is now in full devil form and ready for Marjory to possess.

Sere's plan to thwart the powerful woman goes horribly off course when Marjory takes possession of Sere's body instead of that of the hapless devil she created. With Sere's soul forced back into the computer that spawned her, the devil's daughter finds no other option but to follow the link back to hell. If she can cut Marjory's army off at the source of its power, she might still have a chance of saving the world.

Marjory's army of goblins and half-baked dragons do their best to intercept Sere in hell, but the badass doppelgänger girl has a few tricks up her sleeve for battling them. Getting back out of hell, however, proves far more complex than Sere imagined, requiring the help of not only those she loves but also those she mistrusts. The price for their help will test the limits of Sere's humanity.

*B*ubba's bar reeked of stale beer, man sweat, and the blood of countless brawls. Sere breathed in the rich aromas of life as she pushed open the swinging doors meant to keep the precious cool air inside the establishment.

From behind the bar, Eddie nodded toward the back room. "They're waiting for you."

Sere had been around the bar enough times to know the regulars. "Anything strange happen out in the swamp?" She aimed the question down the counter at anyone who might choose to listen.

One of the bikers leaned in closer to his drink. "You mean other than the six-foot-long crawfish and turtles the size of compact cars?"

"Old news," his companion said. "I haven't seen a good barbeque from Riley's bar in weeks."

The gang traveled the rural highways, which gave them

insight into the goings-on in the small towns. Because few of them made their living out on the water, however, their information regarding the hellmouth was usually incomplete and out of date.

"Keep your eyes open." Sere passed the row of lazy drunks and pushed open the beer-stained wooden door to Bart's office.

The former Navy SEAL sat behind his desk with a glass of Jack and Coke so heavily favoring the alcohol portion that the concoction had only a light tint of color. "We are genuinely fucked, aren't we?"

Though technically not old enough to drink, Doodlebug held an Abita Amber. She stared at the half-empty beer bottle. "All I know is hell, so you tell me."

Sere took a seat at the end of the desk, where a bottle of Jameson whiskey sat next to a half-filled glass. "It's not all gloom and doom. Sanguine is free. She agreed to shut the hellmouth. With the baron's vault closed, that damn iron cage is back in the in-between dimension where it belongs. Since neither Jennifer nor I is inside of it, the Cormorant doesn't have our souls to latch onto in order to haul the vault back into hell's dimension. Only Sanguine knows how to retrieve it."

Bart aimed his glass at her. "But the baron's journals are still out there somewhere."

"That's not even the problem." Doodlebug gave a teenage sneer that made the hairs on the back of Sere's neck stand on end. "What good is sealing the hellmouth after the devil has already escaped? We can't just sit around crying in our glasses."

2

Sere well remembered the doppelgänger-based frustration of longing to fight when all the people around her wanted to talk. "Before we go flying into battle, we need to know what we're up against. You were the last to see Aloysius and his dragon-flying demons. How many were there?"

Doodlebug slammed the bottle down on the desk. "How would I know? As soon as I saw them, Marjory sucked my soul into her computer program."

"Guess."

Bart's controlled tone impressed Sere. He sounded completely unfazed. She, on the other hand, wanted to wring the information out of the doppelgänger girl's throat.

"They filled the sky," Doodlebug said. "I'd say twenty at least. The dragons are still little flamers, not much bigger than ponies. The demons looked a little ridiculous on them, but that doesn't mean they won't be far more impressive on this side of reality."

Sere took a shot of the whiskey. "What about Aloysius? You were part of him becoming the new devil. You must remember something."

Doodlebug drank more of the beer than Sere thought possible for a sixteen-year-old girl. "Not much." She burped out the answer.

Though the girl could annoy goodness out of a saint, Sere had to cut her a break for managing to remember anything at all after being reconstituted in the swamp. "We had to override your system pretty deep with Dooly Buell to bring you back around. Just take it slow and give us what scraps of memory you can scavenge out of the fire pit of your hell-based existence."

Doodlebug chucked the empty bottle into the trash can. "The last thing I remember—other than Lefty carrying my body through the hellmouth—was Aloysius using my spirit to unite the two sides of his being. Unlike what your friend Mr. Fisher experienced, Aloysius's situation isn't a matter of possession." She laced her fingers together. "His human soul and doppelgänger spirit are now one and the same. The really bad part is that Marjory used my connection to the professor's equipment to download all of Aloysius's data into his doppelgänger-computer brain."

"Shit." Sere took another long slug of the whiskey. "Now he truly is an immortal devil. I need to find out from Professor Yates what Aloysius would be using to power his body. With the two sides of himself fused together and all the information he'll ever need stored inside his brain, he can regenerate at will. Is any part of *you* still associated with him?"

Bart reached behind him to the ancient fridge, pulled out a beer, then handed it to Doodlebug, who popped open the bottle by whacking it against the side of the desk. "Not that I can feel."

"There has to be some connection." Bart topped up his drink with more Jack Daniels and a splash of Coke from the can sitting on his desk. "Emotions seem to play a role. My guess is that when Aloysius gets amped up, you might still get a sense of what he's up to."

"We can't rely on that," Sere said. "Doodlebug's role was to be part of the power cord Marjory used to access hell.

Since that bridge is destroyed and the gate shut, whatever connection she had to Aloysius was probably severed as well. Did you get any indication of what happened to the demon horde after they escaped through the hellmouth?"

Bart nodded toward the door. "No one out there has heard anything. I've sent a message down to Riley, but if dragons had flown over her bar, she'd have smoked the tires on her Jeep getting up here. Maybe we got lucky."

Of all the explanations for why demon-horde sightings might have been sparse, *luck* seemed the most improbable. "Demons and dragons didn't have direct connections to life, so Marjory couldn't have used the gate even when it was open," Sere said. "She must have used the vaults in the two dimensions—and the last thin wire of her power cord connecting them."

"If I could have stopped her, I would have." Doodlebug finished off her beer and reached for another, making Sere wonder if her goal was to finish off the whole six-pack.

"No one is blaming you. Marjory outfoxed all of us. The point I was trying to make was she could have used the two vaults as a transporter between dimensions."

Bart kicked his boots up onto his desk. "So down in that bank's basement, there's a devil and his demons and dragons? Sounds like something she'd come up with."

Doodlebug shook her head. "That doesn't feel right. Aloysius didn't trust his great-aunt. He wouldn't have voluntarily stepped back into the vault."

"And with good reason," Bart said. "That woman had no qualms about sacrificing one heir to her dream of immortality, and she certainly wouldn't let another of her

5

clan keep what she thought rightfully belonged to her. Since he is fused together, could he have snuck through the gate before Sanguine closed it?"

"That's possible." Sere looked hard into his eyes. "Speaking of trust, we need to figure out who we can rely on. I had Sanguine slam the door to hell without giving anyone notice. That's not going to sit well with the professor and the others in New Orleans."

Doodlebug turned the bottle in her hand. "Before you go so far as to question your friends' loyalty, maybe you should start a little closer to home. I know you don't trust me."

"Never have, never will," Sere admitted.

"Look, I'm sorry I killed Joe. I know he was your friend."

Sere set her drink down on the desk so hard that whiskey splashed onto the polished wood. "*Sorry* and *friend* are two concepts you don't have any chance of understanding. I'm surprised those words even made it out of your mouth."

Doodlebug's hand moved to the neck of the bottle like she was going to use it as a weapon. "Yet I *do* understand the terms. Maybe you gave me a little too much of Dooly, or maybe it was because the partial regeneration happened in life instead of in hell, but believe me or not, I meant what I said. That's not to imply that I'm asking for forgiveness. You'd never grant it, and I honestly don't care. I did what I did to get your attention. We need each other."

Sere looked at Bart, surprised that he hadn't attempted to quash the argument. "I suppose you're on her side?"

He left his glass on the desk and took a hit straight from the bottle of Jack. "I will always be on your side in all matters, but she does have a point. You don't have to like her to trust her. Hell, you don't even really have to trust her to do anything other than what's in her best interest. Isn't that the way hell works?"

"Maybe so." Sere stared Doodlebug in the eye. "Are you still uncomfortable telling lies?"

The girl didn't break eye contact. "I can tell an untruth if the situation requires it, but I'll never be as smooth as humans. The Cormorant's conditioning runs deep, even for those of us who were never true believers."

In spite of her frustration with the girl, Sere snickered while refilling her glass. "The Cormorant is every bit as conditioned as you think you are—more so actually. You want to know the source of that religious doctrine that rules all doppelgängers? I once saw Jennifer reprimand her son, Bobby. He'd told a fib about some meaningless event that happened at school. She yelled at him, 'We don't tell lies in this house, mister.' Though I don't share her soul the way the Cormorant does, I could feel the waves of firm intention ripple along our connection."

Doodlebug set her bottle down and leaned her elbows on the desk. "You mean to tell me that our doppelgänger dogma about always telling the truth stems from a mother telling her son not to lie?"

Sere shared the doppelgirl's sense of disbelief. "Pretty much. I've often thought that if I hadn't listened to Professor Yates about steering clear of Jennifer, I might have had more influence in her life. If something so simple as a repeated reprimand could influence a self-proclaimed deity, imagine what a little intentional direction could have accomplished."

"Fascinating," Bart said unconvincingly. "But off topic. We still have a devil on the loose, and I doubt the Cormorant is going to be of much help at this stage of the game. She's Sanguine's problem now."

"Right." Sere put her feet up on the desk next to Bart's. "So, Doodlebug has earned conditional trust. What about the professor?"

"He's an old fool." Bart rested his glass on his belt buckle. "But I doubt that man would act against us. It's just not in his nature. I do worry he could be manipulated. Scientists have a bad way of being so enamored with their creations that they don't see the dangers. Were Marjory to send someone in whom he didn't know, he'd probably spill every secret in his enthusiasm for the project."

Doodlebug kept her eyes on her bottle as if the beer's warning label told of some upcoming apocalypse. "So trust his answers, but watch what new information we give him. Is that what you're saying?" Her tone hinted at a suppressed anger.

Sere could tell she was hiding some mistrust, but asking directly would only spin the conversation in another meaningless direction. "It sounds reasonable. You can't possibly expect us to trust you more than we do him."

Doodlebug stared silently at the bottle in the passive-aggressive way only a teenager could achieve—not that Sere cared about the girl's input anyway.

"Polly always impressed me as being a worthy intermediary," Bart said.

Sere sloshed the remaining whiskey in her glass. "She'll make a great inheritor of his creation when the time comes. I guess the bigger question is how far we trust the equipment. Andy messed things up but good when he had control in hell, and Marjory did have her claws in the software." She turned to Doodlebug, hoping to rouse her from her unspoken irritation. "Anything you'd like to share? You were a part of that malware."

"Other than that she'll try again? You already know that." Doodlebug finally leaned back from the desk. "With the gate closed, how much information does the professor have on what's going on with his little puppets?"

"An excellent question," Bart said. "We're still not clear about how Monty first escaped hell. My money is on Andy planting the idea as a way of testing his malware. In any case, that computer system is about as secure as my aunt Sally's garage, and the professor's understandable desire to get a peek at what's happening in hell isn't going to help."

Sere took a drink to calm her nerves. "The computer is a problem, and therefore, working with the people connected to it would only open them up to further attacks from Marjory. What about our voodoo connections?"

Bart stared at her for an unnervingly long time. "Are you opening the door to Baron Samedi?"

She nearly spit out her drink. "Hardly. He has his uses, but I'm actually referring to Kendell, Myles, and their gang. Though they've done heroic work, the more I know, the less I like the seven gates they developed."

"Exactly," Doodlebug said. "I still can't believe one of the portals was inside the bank. How could the people around you be so foolish?"

Sere shrugged. "I wouldn't be so tough on them. It's a long story, and I'm at the center of it. For what it's worth, Sanguine agrees with you. She worries any attempt at opening one of the gates, no matter how well intentioned, will only weaken her ability to keep the hellmouth closed."

Bart leaned so far back in his chair that Sere thought he was searching for an answer on the wood-paneled ceiling. "So if paranormal science and voodoo aren't to be trusted, I guess that brings us to the Wiccan swamp witches. Where did you leave things with Sanguine?"

Seeing her mother figure finally free gave Sere a sense of hope. No one knew more about hell and the tear between dimensions than Sanguine, the creator's granddaughter. "She said she could close the hellmouth, though I don't know how. That access was Wiccan in origin. The gate was how her grandmother, Agnes, transported what she created in life to the other dimension. It was never meant to be used by residents of hell to leave that dimension. My guess is when Sanguine held it open so I could leave, it got stuck, turning what was designed as a one-way gate into the wide-open hellmouth. That's why Lefty has such an easy time swimming through the portal." Sere looked at Doodlebug and Bart, wondering how much to divulge. "Sanguine said if I ever needed to make contact with her now that the hellmouth is closed, I should go through Chloe Aberrant."

"I met her," Doodlebug blurted like a little kid who suddenly had something useful to share. "She created a forty-foot-tall dragon to help me."

"Right," Bart said skeptically.

"No, it's true. She said that by affecting a real person's mental state in life, she could change what the professor's equipment created in hell. Depending on the potion, all manner of ghoulish creatures popped up."

"Wait." Bart lifted his feet off the desk and repositioned them on the floor. He leaned in close to the girl. "So all of those little dragons that Marjory called forth out of hell have human reals?"

"That's what Chloe said." Doodlebug sounded excited, maybe because the new information made her the center of attention. "She said the Laroque mansion is basically a drug den of stoners on her special dragon concoction."

Sere nodded. "Fisher confirmed that Marjory funded a research project that spanned a couple of colleges. We didn't realize she was so far along, though. Having doppelgängers walk through the hellmouth in search of their reals in order to become human-looking demons here in life is one thing. Having them become dragons that fly around in our skies isn't nearly as straightforward."

Bart leaned his head back as if his brain worked best bent over his shoulders. "So far, though, no one's seen any of these dragons."

"Couldn't we just bust in and free the stoners?" Doodlebug asked.

Bart swiveled his chair. "That would be a whole lot easier than breaking into the bank and stealing the vault."

Sere feared they were getting off track. "The dragons are the least of our problems. So long as Marjory is trying to make them real in this dimension, she'll be too preoccupied to continue her immortality endeavor. Our focus has to be on Aloysius Laroque. If we can take him out, Marjory won't have a play. She might be the all-powerful queen on the chessboard, but he's the vulnerable king. After he's dealt with, we can sweep up the other pieces she's been playing with."

"Right." Doodlebug tossed her latest empty bottle into the trash. "Find Aloysius and his demon horde and stop whatever move they intend to make to command the living. Make sure Marjory can't become immortal. Do what we can on this side to ensure that the hellmouth remains closed. Where do we start?"

Bart reached into the top drawer of his desk and pulled out a key with a tiny metal skull fob. "First step is to locate Aloysius. Sere and I will head down to New Orleans and start searching Marjory's strongholds." He tossed Doodlebug the key. "There's a Harley Davidson sportster out back. The dude left it as payment for an especially ugly bar brawl. You won't be setting any speed records with it, but it'll get you from bar to bar. Even though my patrons haven't heard anything, that doesn't mean no one has. Aloysius could be in our midst and somehow keeping the locals quiet. He is, after all, a devil. You're one of the few people who could recognize him. Sit at the counter. Order a soda pop. Do *not* order anything alcoholic. Tell whoever asks that you're searching for your long-lost daddy. Come up with some cover story about him owing your mama ten years' worth of child support. You might ask a question or two with the guys who don't immediately hit on you, but don't push it past casual. Most importantly, listen to the conversations around you."

Doodlebug weighed the key in her palm. "Won't a sixteen-year-old girl stand out in a bar?"

"Not around these parts." Sere nodded over her shoulder. "If you're afraid of the locals, I'm sure we can find you a chaperone from Bart's customers."

Doodlebug clenched the key and stared squint-eyed at Sere. "I'm a demon. Anyone you sent with me would be the one in danger."

Bart got up from behind his desk. "Based on Sere's history, you won't be able to use a cell phone. Work your way south until you get to Joe's cabin. You know where it is. There's a phone inside you can use to call the professor's office if you get into trouble. If you don't find anything, wait there for us to contact you. If you don't hear from us by midnight, head down to the professor's lab, but don't let anyone see you."

SERE STOOD beside Bart as they watched Doodlebug putter the old Harley out of the parking lot. "I don't know if I'm more worried about her safety or that of the people she encounters."

He put his arm around her waist. "Do you think it was a mistake sending her out on her own?"

She relaxed her body against his, grateful to be alone with him. "No. Taking her down to New Orleans would only get the attention of the Laroque clan. She's messed around enough with that family to no longer be our secret weapon. It's taken all we've got to keep Dooly Buell out of their sights. And teeming Doodlebug up with someone here would only result in a bar brawl. She doesn't yet know how to work with others. Hell, I still don't really have that skill down. At times, I barely know how to work with you."

He laughed—a sound that could reawaken her soul from the depths of hell. "You do better than you think. At least she has experience going up against the demons and dragons if she does run into them."

Sere couldn't ignore the dark anguish in the pit of her stomach. "I don't like letting her stay at Joe's cabin."

"I know, but it seemed like the only logical location for stashing her. Hopefully, she'll learn a little humility by camping out in the dead man's bungalow, surrounded by his possessions."

Sere watched the lingering dust kicked up by the motorcycle. "Assuming she makes it that far. Now that the hellmouth is closed, she's adrift when it comes to regeneration. If we hadn't made direct contact between her and Dooly, I don't think she would have recovered."

"I wondered about that." He pulled out the key to his Ducati. "How would the closed gate affect Marjory's little monsters?"

Sere tried to corral the different pieces of information into some coherent idea. "According to Doodlebug, Marjory has the real people who are the basis for the dragons. There would still have to be a connection between real and dragon doppelgänger, and without her bridge of the damned, she can't download the information to make them immortal.

With the reals, however, she can create a direct connection to keep them functional the way we did between Dooly and Doodlebug. That is, assuming the druggies don't overdose or escape. Her demons might be more of a challenge if she doesn't have control of the real people who they're based on. She couldn't have anticipated our closing of the gate, so she might not have chosen the demons with all of the care that she should have. We can't even be sure how many made it out before Sanguine performed her magic."

"Do you think Gerald might be of some use in getting the police force to watch for abductions?" Bart asked.

"I don't know," Sere said. Gerald Laroque, the former chief of police—and grandfather of Aloysius—wasn't someone she was in a hurry to confront in spite of all of his past help.

Bart kneed the four-barrel shotgun holstered at Sere's thigh. "What's your take on those paranormal shells?"

She pulled the key to her Triton from the pocket of her leather pants. "Another very good question. The pellets were meant to sever the connection to hell. Much as I hate to say it, I think our first stop has to be to see the professor. I don't want to confront Aloysius until I know what weapons will work against the devil."

"Do you think Marjory is going to keep her catch under lock and key? If dragons start showing up in the Quarter, things are going to get complicated." He put his hands in his back pockets. The masculine stance made her want to rip his clothes off.

Reluctantly, Sere pulled away from his rock-hard body. "I thought about that too. It's not like Marjory to summon a demon army and leave them languishing in a basement, but turning them loose in the heart of the French Quarter doesn't make much sense either."

"What about the tunnel?"

She tried to visualize the place so she could judge whether it was impregnable. "She must have secured every basement access by now. It would be too out of character for her to leave such vulnerabilities unguarded."

He nodded thoughtfully. "Fisher said Baron Malveaux built it so he could sneak into his brothels unseen. That would mean the access must end in the old Storyville district. Didn't Doodlebug say that area is where she ran into the dragons in hell?"

"Yeah, she said they showed up in the abandoned tenement houses in the Tremé—like that area around the cemetery isn't creepy enough already."

"Better that the demons show up there than appear flying out the bank's front doors. I wonder if the Laroques have any financial interests in the area that might give us a clue about where to look."

Sere began to feel that they were wasting time, but she didn't want to let go of Bart's attention a second sooner than she had to. "I'll have Fisher do some investigating."

Bart finally hopped onto his Ducati. "So first stop, Professor Yates's office. We're just going for a quiet ride along the swamp, okay?"

She pulled on her helmet as she straddled the Triton. "Right. Like that ever happens. Last one to the door buys the next round of drinks."

*S*ere fired up her Triton motorcycle but waited until Bart made the first move. As thorough as her knowledge of the swamp and New Orleans was, when it came to the hidden highways and secluded back roads, he'd beaten her on too many occasions for her to get cocky. *Not this time, my friend. I'm following you until I know I have the advantage.*

When the trail of parking-lot dust kicked up by his back tire reached the toes of her gator-skin boots, she hit the gearshift and laid into the throttle. A hissing from inside her saddlebags accompanied the screech of tires against the gravel. Her two canebrake rattlesnakes stuck their heads out of the flaps like lazy puppies peeking out of their blankets. As the wind picked up over their scales, their tongues emerged to lick at the chase.

"We're going to hang back this time and let him think he's got the advantage, so don't freak out that I'm not taking the lead," Sere told the squirmy reptiles, who never liked it when she didn't give her all to a motorcycle ride. But after Bart made a gentle turn, she heard his engine rev higher, indicating that he was trying to break away, and Sere changed her tune. "Laying back is one thing—giving up is something else." She leaned low over the gas tank of the homemade motorcycle, shifted up a gear, and gave it full throttle. As she crested the curve, she caught the glow of his taillight disappearing around the next bend.

Blasting past Kelly's Diner and Larry's Machine Shop, she felt a familiar lump in her throat. She reminded herself that with Doodlebug's help, the couple had entered the *deep waters*. If there was any justice in the afterlife, the essences of the two would find each other again.

For the run down to Riley's bar, Bart led her along familiar routes—there weren't many side roads that Sere hadn't already explored in her attempts at secrecy, so she was hard to surprise. During the long run along the bayou, he attempted to shed her from his tail more than once, but each time, she maintained her distance.

A long gentle incline had her downshifting to keep him ahead. "Nice try. I'm not letting my eager-demon side take the bait." Learning self-control hadn't come easily, and Bart knew exactly how to draw out her unbridled aggression.

At the outskirts of New Orleans, she held back long enough to be certain he'd lost sight of her. Then instead of sticking to the busy freeway that led into the city, she swung her motorcycle onto an off-ramp that led over the river.

The old Huey P. Long Bridge wasn't for the faint of heart, especially for people on motorcycles. The narrow lanes shook and bounced from the trucks that surrounded her. She had to remain loose to stay in control of the motorcycle on the crowded roadway squeezed between the train trestle and the low railing. Only a hip-high metal bar prevented a dizzying drop to the river below. Sere held onto the handlebars for dear life and focused only on what was in front of her. "I just have to get across the river."

On the downward slope, she opened up the motorcycle like she was on a roller coaster. Darting between trucks and cars, she took the first off-ramp onto the seldom-used road that ran along the winding river. "So long as we don't get stopped by a local cop, we should make it to the Crescent City Connection and back over the river before Bart even makes it through the interchange."

The snakes rattled their tails in approval and admiration of her brilliance.

IN THE EMPTY parking lot of the professor's wharf-side office and laboratory, Sere peeled the helmet off of her sweat- and dust-coated hair just as Bart slid his Ducati to a stop beside her. "That was cheating, you know," he said from under the face shield.

She set her skullcap helmet on the end of her bike's handlebars. "You always say that when you lose."

"Whatever." He pulled off his helmet as he swung his leg from the seat. "How do you want to play this?"

She'd hoped that knowing the root cause of why she felt compelled to always tell the truth would make it easier to overcome the conditioning. It hadn't. She never wanted to lie to Bart, anyway, but when it came to dealing with others, she needed a go-between to prevent her from saying something she shouldn't.

"He's going to have a ton of questions. If I didn't think it would be overly suspicious, I'd wait out here while you found our answers."

"I don't mind taking the lead," he said.

Sere felt unnatural letting other men take the lead, but when it came to Bart, she didn't mind the show of masculine strength. "We need to understand more about the dragons and demons now that the hellmouth is closed—specifically, how to kill them. Hopefully, my scattergun isn't completely useless. If you focus on Aloysius, we might get what we need without divulging too much about what Marjory turned loose. I really don't need those busybodies trying to take charge."

He gave an aggravating smile that made her want to hit him. "Demonsplaining? Really?" He headed off in front of her, giving her ample opportunity to ogle his ass.

"Don't call me a demon," she muttered as she followed him into the offices. She consoled herself with the thought that anyone but Bart would have ended up with a knife in the back for the insult.

Polly threw a large power-supply switch at the back of the hallway. "How about now?"

"Still nothing." Professor Yates was completely focused on his computer screen and didn't acknowledge the visitors.

Bart cleared his throat with entirely too much drama. "I don't mean to interrupt."

The professor finally looked up from the display. "I assume we have you two to thank for this chaos?"

Bart gripped Sere's hand to prevent the buildup of facts from erupting from her mouth. "Sanguine is free, and the hellmouth is closed."

Polly let go of the lever and came out from the shadows. "Well, that must have been some adventure."

Again, Bart squeezed Sere's hand in warning. The good cop-bad cop routine between the professor and Polly was one she'd fallen for too many times. "I'd like to say hell's dangers are behind us, but this might be a matter of closing the barn door after the horse has escaped. Marjory managed to turn her great-nephew, Aloysius, into a full-fledged immortal devil, and he's not alone. We need some answers, and we need them fast, so explanations on our part will have to wait."

Polly sat next to the professor. "Tell us what you need."

Bart finally let go of his iron grip and turned to Sere as if expecting that she'd have everything clearly thought out. She pulled her four-barrel shotgun from her thigh holster and dropped it on the desk. "Is this thing going to do a damn bit of good now that the gate's closed?"

The professor popped one of the shells out of the chamber. He turned the orange plastic sleeve in the sunlight. "Well, the pellets didn't vanish. That's something at least."

"Did you think they would?" Sere couldn't imagine any scenario in which something from hell that had passed through the gate would cease to exist just because the portal had closed.

"I was just spitballing ideas." Polly glared at the professor.

Sere picked up the shotgun, snapped it back together, and reholstered it. "We don't have time for speculative ramblings. Will those pellets work or not?"

The professor lit his pipe, which was never a good sign when Sere was seeking brevity. "So long as the connection between an escaped doppelgänger and their real in life goes through hell, the pellets should work. With the hellmouth closed, however, we have no way of knowing if that's the case, especially with my equipment no longer getting feedback from the dimension. As for a possessed human, between Thomas and Fisher, you've already proven that the pellets can focus and empower the dominant spirit."

"We don't have a case of possession this time," Sere interrupted, not wanting the old man to drone on indefinitely. "Aloysius is bonded into one spirit, and there are monsters with their reals in physical proximity with no access back to hell." She tapped the butt of the gun. "What happens when I shoot them?"

He held his pipe in both hands. "Honestly? I don't know. When it comes to the modified doppelgängers, you could end up killing them by connecting them back to hell with a pellet that originated with Agnes Delarosa's hell, or you could end up empowering them instead."

"Sounds like we need to capture one of the buggers," Bart muttered to Sere.

She nodded but didn't want to pursue the idea around the professor just yet. Since he didn't have a definitive answer regarding the weapon, she chose to move on to her next possible means of combating Marjory. "Which brings up the second question, Professor. Without a tether to hell's computer, how would Marjory power up her little toys?"

The professor aimed his pipe at Polly. "You'd better show them."

Polly pursed her lips while staring at the professor. "A similar problem came up while I was teaching Dooly in life and Doodlebug in hell. The two of them speculated that eventually Doodlebug would join us in life. When that happened, Doodlebug didn't want to be tied to our computer. If I remember correctly, her words were something along the lines of not wanting to be a bitch on a leash."

"What did you do?" Sere asked, suspecting that she wasn't going to like the answer.

Polly pulled a cell phone from the desk. "They each have one of these. Basically, they work like your healing bandage connection to Jennifer, except these can be better regulated and the energy doesn't have to pass through hell. We used the carrier frequency Joe and Bart worked up for your phone—just amped up so it can transfer human energy to a doppelgänger."

The professor aimed his pipe at his bank of computers. "Dooly's is just a normal phone, but because Doodlebug's works on doppelgänger frequency, the signal does pass through my equipment, though I have even less control over what's sent than I have with what transpires between you and Jennifer."

"And does Marjory know about this upgrade?" Sere tried to keep her frustration in check.

"It would be a pretty safe bet," Polly said. "Had we known about Doodlebug's connection to Marjory's bridge of the damned at the time, we might have added in more safeguards."

Bart put his hands in the back pockets of his jeans. "But what Sere does is just a quick infusion of human energy to heal her wounds. We're talking about what a doppelgänger would need for daily living."

Polly nodded. "Dooly already felt like a caged Guinea pig waiting to have more blood drained anytime Doodlebug got hurt. Marjory's marionettes are just as dependent on their reals as Doodlebug is on Dooly. For them to function freely, she would need to have those reals locked away where they could be easily tapped if a doppelgänger got hurt."

Bart's breathing took on a slow, deliberate rhythm as though he was bracing himself for impending danger. "And like a vampire sucking on his victim, a doppelgänger might not know when to stop drinking from its counterpart. Daily blood draws might weaken the real too much for when an actual problem arises."

Sere tried controlling her anger. "That phone doesn't look any different from the one in Bart's pocket."

Polly set the phone down. "As Bart said, we're not talking about the direct real-to-doppelgänger healing energy, just what's needed to survive. Think of it like a plasma transfusion verses needing actual blood. This is just a regular cell phone. Doodlebug doesn't need to call Dooly for a quick pick-me-up. Anyone would do. She just needs the app running when someone answers. The conversation doesn't even have to last all that long."

Bart pulled out his phone and stared at it like it was about to sprout fangs. "So a call about my vehicle's expired warranty could actually be a soul-sucking doppelgänger on the other end, looking for a quick fix of human energy? No wonder those calls always leave me on edge."

"That's what we came up with, and we're not all that devious compared to Marjory Laroque."

Sere wondered why they'd even bothered visiting the professor, but then, if she'd wanted something to make her feel better about her life, she'd have stayed in bed with Bart. "Do you have any good news at all?"

The professor nodded toward his equipment. "If we can't check on hell, neither can Marjory. That means Sanguine will be dealing with the residents of hell without human interference, which has to help. Can you give me any information on what's happening on the other side of the gate?"

Sere wished she had better news. "Nothing you don't probably already know. Sanguine plans on rehabilitating Jenna, but convincing the birdwoman to lay down the *god* title sounds all but hopeless to me. Is Jenna still powered by Jennifer?"

The professor got out of his chair and flipped on the virtual diorama of hell's New Orleans. The translucent images looked like ghosts. "The projection is stable, so the people being modeled in life still have their information sent to the doppelgängers in hell. This hologram only shows where the mirror images *should* be, though, not where they actually are. As we know from Monty, that makes this little marionette stage all but useless. All I can tell you is that the information, including Jenna's, is still being transmitted."

Polly pointed at the virtual representation of the thirty-three-story tower by the river. "So long as the World Trade Center continues pumping out energy, we need to continue using the power to prevent another runaway reaction."

"I'm more than familiar with the problem," Sere said. "What you're saying is that the realm is stable, at least as near as you can tell, and the Cormorant is unaffected by the closed gate."

"That's it in hell's nutshell," the professor said.

SERE HELD Bart's hand as they walked back to the bikes. "I've been thinking about what you said. You're right. We need to capture one of Marjory's demons, though a dragon might be even better."

"What do you have in mind?"

She grabbed her helmet off the bike's handlebars. "I keep circling back to our idea about the tunnel that leads into the bank's basement. Even if Marjory has all of the side entrances sealed or guarded, that shaft has to go somewhere. I think I'll head over to Fisher's office."

Bart straddled his Ducati before grabbing his helmet. "That will give me time to swing by Joe's old cache and grab some weapons. Even if Marjory doesn't have a militia hanging out in the tunnel, if we're right about her demon army being sequestered in the basement, we'll need all the firepower we can get. At least we'll have the benefit of constrained access. Those dragons won't be able to fill the tunnel with fire if only one can stick his head in at a time. Now that we have a little more information, what do you think about making contact with Gerald?"

She knew she'd have to approach the old man at some point, but without even a clue as to the demon army's location, she wasn't ready to cross that bridge just yet. Sere fired up her Triton. "We've got enough to deal with at the moment. If he makes contact, I won't avoid him, but we need to figure out what we're up against before dragging him into it."

Bart gave her a curt nod before revving his engine then headed down the road. She had the urge to follow him, but it didn't last. Though Joe's old haunts still calmed her soul, melancholy would inevitably take over. She turned the motorcycle toward the French Quarter and left the professor's lab in the dust.

THE RUN from the professor's lab to Fisher's CPA office had become so well traveled that even the homeless population had stopped harassing Sere with their usual banter. She parked in the back alley next to a dude who'd created a bed from milk crates. "What's the word on the street, Lester?"

"Strange sounds from under the bank late last night, but who ya gonna believe?"

She dropped him a dollar. "Watch my motorcycle."

"I always do." He stashed the bill in his tattered shirt.

As Sere pushed open the door, Linda barely looked up

from her computer. "I'm not even going to ask." She buzzed Fisher as Sere headed for his door.

As usual, the desk in the office was covered in receipts, but that had never stopped Fisher from pushing everything aside the moment she walked in. "What eruption from hell are you dealing with today, superhero?"

She angled her shotgun away from the chair as she collapsed into it. "What do you know about that tunnel that led into the bank's basement?"

He pulled a key from his waistcoat and used it to unlock the bottom drawer of his desk. "I figured eventually you'd be looking for a way back into that shaft, so I did a little digging in the New Orleans Historic Collection. When the city had Storyville razed, they annexed part of the property to expand the cemetery. Your father wasn't in any position to buck the puritanical tide, but he did manage to secure a couple of the new grave sites." He pulled a copy of a bill of sale from the file folder and slid it across the desk to Sere.

"So this is the back door to the bank's basement?" The map of the cemetery grounds listed each of the plots by number. A handwritten scrawl at the bottom indicated the ones the baron had purchased.

"I'm not sure I'd go that far." Fisher thumbed through the file before pulling out a couple of photocopied newspaper obituaries. "The baron might have intended to create an escape route, but he didn't bother telling any of his heirs. Over the last hundred and fifty years, a number of your kin have found their final resting places on those plots." He handed over a dozen pictures that looked to have been recently taken. "After compiling the data, I took a tour of the grounds. From the engravings on the headstones, it's clear that each of the crypts has been well used."

Sere leaned back in the chair and examined the photos. "If there's a secret passage, Marjory would have had a challenge creating an entrance with all of her ancestors clogging up the crypt."

"It's not impossible. She certainly would have had someone walk to the end of the tunnel, but any aboveground work would have been recorded. There is a piece of good news—even with her considerable financial power, she hasn't been able to buy every building that lines Conti Street, though at present, I haven't found any construction sites that might provide access to the tunnel."

Sere continued to look at the aboveground crypts. "Even without owning the buildings, Bart and I figured Marjory would have bricked up the tunnel from inside."

In his seersucker suit, Fisher looked far too respectable for the work she kept assigning to him. "That would make sense. The receipts for the basement remodel after your run-in with her last devil seemed suspiciously high. Still, so long as contractors look for basement drainage, they'll be punching holes to access that tunnel. What are you planning to do?"

Unlike the professor, Sere never minded Fisher's questions. More often than not, giving him information had ultimately resulted in her being rescued. "It's less about what I have in mind than about trying to anticipate Marjory's next move. If I'm right about her having a basement full of demons and dragons, she wouldn't want to let them out through the teller windows. Having visible demons in the institution wouldn't do much for business. She's going to need a way to get them out without connecting them to her bank. It might be time to see if there have been any recent burials in the cemetery. She wouldn't necessarily need one of the family plots, just a tomb with a deep enough ancestor pit to reach the tunnel."

He closed the drawer, locked it, and returned the key to his pocket. "What do you think she'll use her new pets for? She already controls most of the city. You make it sound like she's preparing for an attack."

"Maybe she is. So far, she seems to think one step ahead of us. According to Doodlebug, there was a war brewing in hell."

Fisher leaned forward over his desk. "I know that everyone thinks with the hellmouth closed that communication has been cut, but do *you* believe that when it comes to Marjory?"

"I think if Marjory and Madam Laroque were standing in front of us, it would be impossible to tell the difference. Every real that I've met has shared a mutual mistrust with the corresponding marionette. The instinctual assumption is that hell's puppets want to take command of the real people who inspire them. That's usually enough to keep the two sides apart. However, I don't believe that's the case with Marjory and her double. I think they work in tandem. Even if they can't talk to each other, they would still stick with the plan."

"Sanguine is going to have her hands full."

She smiled at Fisher, but she was worried about exactly that—eventually, Sanguine was going to need help. Sere pocketed the map and pictures. "I'll need to talk to Bart, but I think the most logical play is for us to sneak into the cemetery tonight. If we can find an access, we'll work our way down the tunnel. You've performed some impressive financial magic in the past, so anything you can do to help keep us out of Marjory's clutches would be a big help."

He swiped the receipts off the table and into a box. "I'm on it."

3

*S*ere checked her analog army watch. "With the hellmouth closed, midnight should just be another tick of the clock, but my guess is those demons would feel right at home at that hour. If we're going to snag one outside of Marjory's cave, this would be the time."

Next to her, Bart pressed against the cemetery's brick wall with knives and guns stashed around his body. "So, what's your plan?"

She peeked through the wrought-iron gate. Only shadows played between the crypts. "Though I'd like to see what's going on in that bank's basement, what we really need to do is to entice one of the monsters out of its hiding spot. I'd rather not kick over the whole hornets' nest until we have some idea of what we're dealing with."

He looked at her, eyebrows raised in surprise. "That's a remarkably reasonable approach. I half expected you to say we were going to conduct a full-out assault on the bank stronghold." He made a quick scan of the grounds then ducked his head back into the shadows. "If I had a squad in hiding, I'd post a sentry somewhere they couldn't be seen."

She pressed harder to the wall to avoid a set of passing headlights. Even in their black riding leathers, she and Bart could still be visible to every eye in the neighborhood. She rested her hand on the butt of her shotgun for reassurance. "You're the expert. Where do we look for the demon bastard?"

He knelt down and picked up a stick. Drawing a series of boxes in the dirt, he quickly rendered a map of the grounds. "A skilled commando wouldn't want to hang around the entrance to the camp. He'd want to be far enough away that an invading force wouldn't immediately know where to attack but close enough that he could skedaddle back to base if he saw trouble. He'd act as sentry, not engaging with the enemy but also not alerting his forces until he was sure there was a threat."

She pointed at the cemetery entrance on the drawing. "We know the baron's crypts are toward the back of the grounds. Our prey would want to be close enough to the gate to see it but remain hidden from anyone passing by. That means he probably wouldn't have a perfect lookout. Do you think he'd be on top of one of the tombs? As a demon, he might try to pass as a carved gargoyle."

Bart shook his head. "He would need to maintain an easy access to his forces. My bet is he'd be behind one of these two mausoleums along the second street of the dead. That would keep him in the shadows from the front gate, give him a running start back to his buddies, and involve minimal wandering around for him to keep an eye on things."

Sere made a mark where Bart had indicated. "So we'll need to get behind him if we want to capture him before he calls out his demon friends. I've gotta say, Marjory couldn't have done a better job of picking an access point for her monsters if she'd designed it herself. No one goes poking around cemeteries at night."

Bart got up and returned to the shadows of the wall's irregularities. "And even if someone does go there, who's going to go blabbing about seeing a monster among the tombs?"

Sere studied the map. "If we knew which structure he was behind, we could sneak past him. His line of sight on the gate has to be restricted."

Bart scanned the top of the crumbling brick-and-plaster wall. "There might be a less obvious way around him. With one good hoist, I'll bet I could throw you up to the top of this wall. You could wait there until I approach the front gate. While his eyes were on me, you could hop down and make your move."

The reckless part of Sere savored the plan. With the iron gate between them, the demon wouldn't be a threat to Bart. But her more cautious side made her ambivalent. When she worked with other people, however, they tended to get hurt. "You would honestly just stand there and let me take him down?"

He gave a sly smile. "I wouldn't say *that*. I've been known to scale iron bars before. Either our prey turns on you and I get him, or he comes after me, leaving you to attack."

"Or he does what you explained and heads hell-for-leather back to his buddies. But I suppose that's where I intercept him. Okay. I don't see a better plan. Just, please don't twist your ankle or do anything stupid."

"Look who's talking. Give me your foot, and I'll hoist you up."

She put her hands on his broad shoulders and lifted her gator-skin boot to his waiting hands. Her hop off the ground felt like it had been spring-loaded. She landed on hands and knees like a cat on top of the brick wall. If the demon had spotted her, he didn't make a fuss about it. *Must be plenty of owls, rats, and other night creatures to ignore on a night like this.*

A patch of clouds moved off, allowing the moonlight to bathe the grounds. She lay flat on the top of the wall and let her eyes respond to any movement below. If there was a demon down there, he wasn't the run-of-the-mill idiot she'd dealt with in the past.

Out of the corner of her eye, she spotted Bart's hulky figure looming around the front gate like a tourist who didn't know better than to poke his nose where it didn't belong. She did her best to remain focused on the cemetery grounds. *Come on, you asshole, show yourself. I've never known Bart to be wrong about military tactics, and Marjory isn't stupid. She wouldn't bring a platoon of demons and dragons across from hell then leave them unprotected.*

Bart scaled the gate by grabbing the iron bars and pressing his feet to the brick wall. If Sere hadn't known he was trying to attract the attention of a demon, she would have thought he was making a covert incursion. His jump to the ground, however, was loud enough to call forth any sentry. She remained hidden on top of the wall while he darted behind the nearest tomb.

Even though I can't see the bastard, I can't stay up here all night. If Bart's right, which he almost always is, our demon prey could be running through the shadows to raise the alarm while I lie here like an idiot. Sere eased her legs off the ledge and held onto the lip to avoid a noisy entrance like the one Bart had made. She let go and landed with bent knees to cushion the impact.

Darkness was a friend to Sere, but any demon accustomed to the forever night of hell would be equally at home in the shadows. She pulled the knife from her boot. Her prey would either be holding his vigil, creeping up on Bart to investigate, or slinking back toward the tunnel opening. If the idiot was too dense not to have heard Bart's landing, the former Navy SEAL would flush him out soon enough. Bart could take care of himself, which meant circling around to help would only result in a firm chastisement. The bigger threat was that the demon might already be working his way toward the rear of the cemetery.

Sere crept past the first crypt then gazed down the long pathway. Not even a rat could be seen moving in the shadows, so she hurried to the next road in the city of the dead—again, nothing. *This is stupid. He could be running full speed toward the far end of the grounds.* She hustled to the next passage but took a more cursory glance to be sure she wasn't seen.

As she crossed from the old section of cemetery to the relatively newer area, she stopped pretending to search for the demon. If he was this far back, he'd already detected the invaders. She turned down the marble-strewn path toward the closest of Baron Malveaux's crypts listed on Fisher's map. As she passed the polished marble door with its carved cherubs and demons, she gave it a firm pat to ensure that it was sealed. Darting back toward the end of the cemetery, she focused on the tombs. *Four down and two over.*

She overshot her mental map. As she turned back, a blanket covered her face as if she'd run into the dense fabric drying on a line. She swung at it with her knife, hoping to skewer whatever attacker had lain in wait. Instead, a hand grabbed her wrist and twisted it behind her. A foot kicked her behind the knee, forcing her to the ground. She fought against the wool as if it were the one doing the attacking, but ropes wound around her torso and limbs then tightened like nooses before a hanging. The ground rasped under her until the jagged rocks were left behind. Smooth marble indicated that she was no longer out in the open. A low rock rumble announced the closing of the crypt.

4

*A*s Sere felt the regular, thumping splat of each wet brick in the tunnel against her bound body, her primary worry was that Bart would do something stupid like try to rescue her. Of course, he would have to do something, but Bart going in alone and emotional would only land both of them in Marjory's hands. After what felt like hours, the ground under the soggy blanket wrapped around her transitioned from moldy bricks to the familiar concrete of the bank's basement. The brute hauling her by her feet dropped his load.

The blanket was pulled from her face, revealing Marjory Laroque, who looked at her smugly. "I really expected catching you to be considerably harder."

Sere spit the taste of wool, dust, and corpses from her mouth. "There had to be easier ways to arrange a meeting."

"Oh, I think the time for talking is over. Look around you. You've lost."

Sere stared up at the two hulking brutes who'd abducted her. Based on their girth and strength, they were clearly of Gerald's linage. The lack of redness in the eyes and their tanned skin made it clear they weren't demons from hell.

"I would have thought you'd rely on your new militia."

Marjory backed up and waved at the cages behind her. Dragons huffed and paced around the floor-to-ceiling metal prison cells like dogs in a shelter. In front of each enclosure sat a demon wearing a collar and a leash. "You mean my prize possessions? I wouldn't dare risk losing even one."

"I don't get it," Sere said. "Why bring forth an army of the damned just to imprison them?"

Marjory leaned on her cane and shook her head. "You really are full of yourself, aren't you? You think I did all of this just to do battle with you and your friends? These are my test subjects."

Sere rolled back against the floor to glare at the woman. "You can't possibly still be trying to create an immortal. The hellmouth is closed and your bridge of the damned destroyed. All you've got left is that iron box, but without a way to power it, you might as well use it to store your antiques. Like it or not, Aloysius was the closest you came to success. Where is that devil, anyway?"

"Safely away from you and your little marble pellets. You think I didn't figure out how you destroyed my sweet Devlin? That stupid little rock was all that was left when he turned to dust."

Sere smiled. "You played your hand, and I played mine."

"You may have won that battle, but this room will be the

scene of your ultimate defeat. I have everything I need from your foolish dimension right here."

Sere tried putting together the puzzle pieces Marjory clearly believed she'd collected. "What makes you think that just because you have some of hell's creations you can make yourself immortal? From what I can see, you don't even have your personal doppelgänger. If I were more versed in the subtleties of deceit, I'd say you were bluffing."

Marjory held her cane to her side. "Why would I want to spend all of eternity in this old body when you're proof that I don't have to?"

"So you're planning on taking *my* body?" Sere wondered why the powerful seemed drawn to Jennifer's homemaker image.

"I'll use you if I have to, but you're not my first choice. I don't relish being a squeaky little redheaded girl. Your soul, however, is as powerful as that of anyone I've ever met, with the possible exception of your father." She towered over Sere. "Our family connection should make it easier for me to tap into your spiritual energy the way Aloysius did with Doodlebug. You're my power source."

"So you believe I'm the connection to hell that you need for making your immortals?"

"Not just you." She turned to the cages. "Those beasts weren't meant simply to fly my family's doppelgängers out to the vaults. My immortal heirs will have the hearts of dragons as those beasts are crushed in my vault to release their power."

"You can knock on hell's door all you want, but the gate is still closed. Even the professor can't tell what's happening in that dimension. You may have that stupid vault, but you still lose."

Marjory walked back to the table then picked up the baron's old journal. "Then you and I will have to find a way of opening it. Your father had some interesting ideas on possessing another's body. I know firsthand how successful he was with Myles Garrison."

Sere wished she could sit up so she could spit on the woman. "Do you honestly believe you could fool those around me into helping you?"

"No. The baron was an expert manipulator, and even he didn't bother trying to convince others he was still the foolish bartender. I've seen the lengths those around you will go to rescue you or help you with your cause. When the fools see that you've been possessed, I expect superhero antics from them in their attempt to save you." She leaned down over Sere. "And we both know where you belong. To get me out of you, your spirit will have to make the journey back to hell. The door may be locked, but with you, I have the key."

OF ALL OF Sere's fears, being driven from her body ranked the highest. From day one, the nascent spirit of Jenna had wanted the return of her doppelgänger form. As the Cormorant, Jenna had found a more impressive presentation—one that inspired religious awe in her followers. With Jennifer's mirror ruling hell, Sere had even less incentive to return to the cursed dimension. So long as Sere remained among the living, Jenna couldn't reach her.

Baron Samedi and the other loas of the dead had made it clear that her soul belonged to them and living in the reproduction form was an abomination in their eyes. The spectral spirits of death had haunted her from the shadows throughout her existence, though she'd won a reprieve from them by rescuing the souls Marjory had stolen. How long that consideration would last was a question that plagued her.

Hunched in the corner of the vault, still bound, Sere wondered what would really happen when Marjory closed the door. Though there wasn't anything she could do to defend herself physically, she did still have options spiritually. "You do realize any sane scientist wouldn't experiment on herself."

Marjory consulted the journal then set it back on the table. "I think we can both assume that sanity doesn't really play a part in anything the baron devised." She entered the vault and pulled the locking wheel behind her.

The smells of old iron, singed electronics, and ancient curses teased at Sere's doppelgänger nose. Her body responded to the sensations by making her vomit. The last time she'd been in one of the iron boxes, Sere wasn't the one processing the physical inputs to her senses—Jenna had done that, and Sere had been just about to steal the doppelganger girl's body.

"Fuck you, Father."

Marjory kicked Sere onto her stomach. "There's not much point in keeping you tied up. I'd hate to have to wait for others to free me before making my grand debut. The energy should start flowing between us any moment now."

"Unless you fucked up. Tell me, what exactly makes you think you're going to be the dominant force in this unwanted union?"

Marjory yanked at the knots with her arthritic fingers. "In case you hadn't noticed, I'm used to getting what I want."

Every hair on Sere's arms and legs stood on end. Her eyes stung. A loud buzzing that felt like it was coming from inside her head made her wish she could jab a knife in her ears. Her hands were free, but all she could use them for was to cover her face. The acrid smell of voodoo potions not only penetrated her nose but oozed down the back of her throat as well. Sere could just make out Marjory's screaming past the growing clamor in her head. She recognized it as a reaction to the transfer.

The soul of Marjory Laroque loomed over Sere's consciousness, attempting to invade her against her will. "I'll take what's mine."

"The hell you will!" Sere screamed. She sought her memories for Joe's teachings. Her fighting mentor, father figure, and friend had taught her all manner of combat preparedness, both physical and mental.

"That's right, retreat into your memories," Marjory said.

The view shifted as Sere's eyes swept the vault, but she wasn't the one moving the muscles. *If you can't win, retreat to a place you can defend, and regroup. Just because you've ceded the ground to your enemy, that doesn't mean they won't still have to work to command it. Just don't take forever in your counterattack.* The memory of Joe's lecture after an especially humiliating defeat by him made her feel like a child sitting in front of her teacher.

Though Sere's body still belonged to her, Marjory's understanding of the baron's writings threatened that tenuous control. Sere felt destined to lose the battle with the woman. Marjory, however, wouldn't know there was a trap door Sere could escape through.

THE INSIDE of the computer was as hard, cold, and calculating as the professor himself. Sere's primary consolation was that if Marjory chose to chase her into the software, she'd be trapped like a rat in a cage, where escape was only possible if the mechanism could be deciphered. *Fuck, I'm even starting to think like a computer.* As always, swearing provided a good way for Sere to hang onto her humanity.

She took a moment to orient her perceptions. Every computer connected to the professor's equipment had its own camera, so *seeing* was disorienting but simple enough to understand. Similarly, *hearing* could be deciphered so long as she focused on only one input at a time. Her senses of smell, touch, and taste remained grounded in the vault. *At least I still have those connections to my body.*

She focused on the screen displaying Polly Urethane hard at work. The computation regarding a search for lost doppelgängers would take weeks at the speed the woman was going, but Sere guessed that having anything to do beat sitting idle. "Um, excuse me."

Polly jumped out of her chair and stared at the screen like it was possessed. "What's going on?"

"Sorry, Polly. It's me, Sere. We've got a problem. Marjory has infiltrated my body. My only escape was into the computer software. I didn't mean to scare you."

Polly hurried back to her seat. "Shit. What do you need me to do?"

"Get everyone rounded up—Bart, Kendell, Doodlebug, anyone you can haul in on short notice. Call Bart first. He was with me on our adventure. I don't need him trying to do something heroic and making things worse. I know it's early." One advantage of being mostly computer was that Sere didn't need to consult her watch to know the time. At least those working at the Scratchy Dog wouldn't mind the early hour. While early morning might mean the start of the day for most, Myles and Kendell would still be cleaning up after a long night.

"Are you okay?"

Sere had known that would be the first question everyone would ask. "I'm in contact with my body. It's still in the vault under the bank, but I don't expect Marjory to be hiding out forever. Once she feels she has control over the limbs and realizes I'm not sitting in wait for a counterattack, she'll open the box."

"So we don't have much time." Polly pulled out her sugar skull-covered cell phone. "Bart, it's Polly. Sere's soul is here with me in the computers. She's mostly okay. She says get that hot ass moving. We've got trouble."

Sere tried to laugh, but the computer had trouble processing the reaction. While Polly made contact with the others, Sere investigated her digital surroundings. The computers continued gathering data from all points of the map surrounding New Orleans, but only those people who'd been residents for six months had the information uploaded to the professor's hell cloud. From there, the basis of every doppelgänger disappeared like rain emanating from hell's hurricane. An entire bank of computers sat idle, waiting for some hint of what was happening in the foreign dimension. The whole process still mystified her.

"Hey, kiddo." The professor sat in his old Barcalounger, wearing pajamas and an old robe. He hadn't called her that in years.

"Do you even go home anymore?" she asked.

"And miss out on the latest impending apocalypse? Not on your immortal life. So, what does our dear Marjory Laroque think she's up to this time?" He pulled out his pipe and started the ritual of cleaning it.

Sere checked to be sure Polly had finished her calls for help. "Marjory believes that if she takes a real and their doppelgänger then crushes another doppelgänger with a direct link to the computer—like Doodlebug—she'll be able to access your stored data and download it to the doppelgänger brain."

Polly drew out the idea in stick figures the way the professor often did. "But Doodlebug was unique. She was part of Marjory's malware demonic bridge of the damned. Now that she's on this side, Marjory couldn't use her again."

"She doesn't need to," the professor said. "Those dragons of hers aren't the direct creation of our equipment."

"So the dragons are a result of the malware?" Polly asked as Doodlebug snuck into the office. The computer's silent alarm went off at the doppelgänger intrusion.

"Yes. They create a back door into my equipment."

Doodlebug stood behind Polly. "Chloe said they were the result of a drug concoction fed to their reals."

"But how are the dragons continuing to exist with the hellmouth closed?" Sere asked.

"The same way you do." The professor pulled out a button from his shirt. "Sanguine might be the blockage to the gate, but Jennifer, Jenna, and you are the thread that runs through the hole in the center of the button. It would appear that Marjory has found a way to punch more threads through the hole."

"Then there are other mirrors in hell like Jenna?" Sere asked.

Professor Yates refastened the top button of his cotton pajama shirt. "It would be worth investigating, assuming we had the resources in hell."

Bart burst through the door so hard that Sere was surprised it hadn't shattered. He looked around the room in confusion. "Where is she?"

Polly got out of her chair then put her hand against his chest. "Calm down. She's okay, but Marjory has control of her body."

Kendell and Myles came in just as Polly finished her sentence. "I don't see how that's *okay*, Polly," Kendell said in a tone that matched Bart's.

"I'm right here," Sere said, using every speaker in the office. "I need you all to take a breath while we figure out our next move."

"Our next move is obvious," Bart said. "We have to get you out of that computer and back into your body. The longer Marjory has control of it, the harder the exorcism."

"Before we go off half-cocked," Doodlebug said, "why does she even *want* Sere's body?"

Sere really wished she could form a fist and hit something. "She is using me as bait in a trap. Ultimately, she wants the hellmouth reopened. She figures if I can't or won't do it, you all will to do it to save me. So far, I've played right into her hands by occupying the computer, but I didn't see any other choice."

Bart leaned over the closest monitor. "This isn't what we planned. I've spent the last hour pulling apart tombs, searching for you."

Sere tried to snicker, and again, the computer had trouble figuring it out. "I'm sorry. The whole thing was a setup. She didn't even have any of the demons outside of the basement, just her henchmen waiting for me to spring the trap. I'm glad they didn't snag you as well. Now, can we focus on what we need to do?"

"If I said no, would it make a difference?" Bart glared into the screen.

She couldn't blame him for his display of emotion. If their roles had been reversed, she'd be far less understanding. "We have to go through this problem to get me back to being whole. From Marjory's description of using doppelgängers and reals to create immortals, I believed her when she said she had everything she needed. But now that I'm in this computer, I'm beginning to wonder if there's something missing."

The professor finally looked up from his computer. "To begin with, she doesn't have her doppelgänger body."

Sere blinked the computers on either side of the room as her way of shaking her head. "She said she doesn't want to be an old lady for all of eternity."

"Doesn't matter." The professor turned to his ever-present pad of paper. "Unlike you, Marjory is starting off with a physical body. She can't just abandon it. The only two possessions the baron accomplished both started out with an unencumbered soul—both his spirit and yours having come from Guinee. We have plenty of examples of doppelgänger spirits trying to take over their humans' bodies, but when it comes to a foreign human spirit occupying a doppelgänger body, there's only Sere."

"And now Marjory," Sere said.

The professor shook his pen at the computer screen. "Not really. Marjory's body must be kept safe. She is still tethered to it, as you must still be connected to yours."

"How do you figure?" Bart asked.

Kendell crossed her arms. "To start with, we haven't been visited by Baron Samedi. If Marjory's body had died, he'd be poking around, searching for the lost soul. Ever since the demons collected the spirits for that woman's interdimensional bridge, that loa of the dead has been keeping a more watchful eye on events."

"You're all making my head hurt." Doodlebug took the pen from the professor and jabbed it onto the page.

"Marjory has an actual body." She jabbed the pen on the hell side of the professor's drawing. "She needs her doppelgänger, either as a mirror in hell or the actual body in life—which one, we don't know. But either way, she needs to make contact with her hell self." She drew a big question mark back to reality. "So either the damned version of her spirit acts as a mirror—which would only work if it were encapsulated in these fucking computers— and she hauls her bony puppet's ass back here for her eternal use, or she leaves her doppelgänger where it is and occupies another marionette. Even the baron's journals can't explain that trick, as he never had to deal with his original form. Have I got that about right?"

The professor took his pen back and inspected the crushed tip. Then he threw it away and grabbed another from the coffee cup on his desk. "No one said the calculation was simple."

Polly hadn't stopped pacing since the others had arrived. "Aloysius's soul traveled down the cord from life to hell. Presumably, his body is rotting in some swamp. Using Doodlebug's connection to our equipment, Marjory united human soul to doppelgänger spirit, thus allowing the united being to exist in the puppet body. Doodlebug's connection was the key. Without that, she wouldn't have been able to access our data on the doppelgänger body and thereby allow him to regenerate at will."

"I'm with you so far," Bart said.

Polly pointed her chewed fingernail at the screen. "She thinks she can use Sere's soul in the same manner. Doodlebug was right. Why does she want Sere's body?

Marjory knows her process only works if she uses her own double."

Sere's scream of frustration blew out a section of computer monitors. "And now I'm inside the computer—one step closer to giving her exactly what she wants."

"But the step is out of order." Bart pushed off of his position against the wall. "Without making contact with her doppelgänger self, she has no play. What is she expecting?"

Sere knew he wasn't going to like her answer. "For me to go to hell. *That's* where the battle will be. With Sanguine distracted by the Cormorant, Madam Laroque will think she has control. It will be a race to see who can open the gate first. Marjory said I was the key, but Sanguine is the lock."

"Then don't go to hell." Bart glared at the screen.

"Then Sere abandons her body to Marjory." Polly kept pacing while chewing another fingernail. "Even tethered to her real body, Marjory could live indefinitely inside of Sere. She'd just need to leave her real body in the interdimensional vault, where it wouldn't age. And Bart's right. The longer Sere hides out in these computers, the harder it will be to drive Marjory out of her body."

"But what good would it do Sere to go to hell?" Bart asked.

"Marjory doesn't really want to live in my body," Sere said. "This was just her opening gambit. She wants all of her heirs to become immortal along with her, which means she's ultimately going to need to get her body out of the vault so she can use it again. She needs not merely to unite real and doppelgänger but to do it by passing the mirror through hell. In hell, I can stop that from happening."

"How?" he asked. "You're nothing more than a ghost in a machine."

"By uniting Sanguine and Jenna in our cause. Hell needs someone to rule over it, and we can't let that be Madam Laroque. Without my help, Sanguine is about to be blindsided and challenged for control."

Doodlebug bit her lip. "Living Marjory wouldn't even need to make contact for that to happen. The two Madams Laroque don't have the usual doppelgänger-real mistrust—they practically think with one mind. Certainly, when it comes to ruling hell, either version would love to be at the controls."

Sere leaned back into the constantly running computations. "So I sit here, and Marjory takes control of hell, abducts Sanguine, and breaks open the hellmouth. Or I go to hell to join the battle and risk being used as the key that opens the gate."

Bart fell into the chair. "Like that's even a choice for you. Okay. So Sere goes to hell. How do we help?"

"First, it's not that easy." The professor waved at his equipment. "I'm not the one who sealed the gate shut. For Sere to change dimensions, we're going to need some non-paranormal-science magic to clear the way. The original gate was Wiccan in origin. Anyone know how to find Chloe Aberrant?"

*D*oodlebug had been out to the swamp enough times to know more or less where Chloe lived. Flying on the back of a dragon or creeping through the vegetation at midnight during a hurricane, however, were radically different from riding on a Harley in broad daylight. The old engine made a *poke-poke* sound, mirroring the vibration that shook her from feet to fingers. She missed the high-performance Honda Blackbird. The sun made her squint under the full-face helmet Bart insisted she wear.

"Like I would really get hurt falling off this slow-moving motor scooter." She pushed the visor up for better visibility. The lack of rain and incessantly bright light made her feel like she was on display to any adversary that might be lurking among the trees.

As she entered a small town, she knew she'd made a wrong turn somewhere. During Smoke's flights, she'd never seen any habitations. "Shit." She couldn't even pull over and ask directions. Even if any of the townsfolk did know about the swamp witch, they'd probably refrain from handing out directions, for fear of being cursed.

Doodlebug took the first left that she came to that veered away from the Mississippi River. "I know she's inland, and I know she's still farther away from New Orleans."

For the next hour, she took turns at random, relying more on instinct than memory. When the Harley finally ran out of gas, she coasted it to the side of the dirt road. She'd have been happy to toss the useless motorcycle into the river, but she still needed a way to get home.

"Who ever heard of a motorcycle running out of gas? Jeez!" She got off the bike and threw the helmet on the ground next to the front tire. "Hopefully, Chloe knows how to brew up something that will make you run."

Doodlebug headed into the cypress forest without a clue as to where she was or how to find the swamp witch. "Why does life have to be so damn confusing?" A low growl made her spin around and search the tree limbs. "Midnight? Is that you? I could really use your help if you're around."

The black panther lumbered down from his perch in the tree, but he only stared at her without leading the way.

"It's me, Doodlebug. You led me to your mistress in hell. Do you remember?"

He blinked at her and turned toward the forest. Even in the light of day, his dark coat so easily meshed with the shadows that she dared not take her eyes off him as she followed. The trees, vines, and streams were every bit as confusing in life as they'd been in hell. At a large river, he stopped and lapped at the water while she remained in the shadows.

"Hey, boy." The man's voice made her heart flutter.

"Bernie?"

The strapping twentysomething dude who played the real for the dragon named Smoke rose from the river's edge. He had a handful of plant stalks. "I'm Bernie. Do we know each other?"

"I'm Doodlebug."

He walked around her. His inspection made her intensely self-conscious. "So you're the one who's caused me so many hungover mornings. I thought you were consigned to hell."

"Clearly, I'm out. You must be seriously out of touch. I need to find your owner."

"You mean Chloe? She's hardly my owner."

Doodlebug wasn't in the mood to debate semantics. "Whatever. I need to find her. Are we far from her cabin?"

He nodded toward the other side of the river. "A couple of miles as the dragon flies. A couple of hours by foot."

"Too bad you can't transform in life the way you can in hell. Lead on."

He rested his fists, filled with stalks, against his hips. "I've still got work to do. If you want to help, we can get it done sooner. Otherwise, you can start hiking."

"Look. I'm not out here for the fun of it. Sere's in trouble, and I need to find Chloe right now. Why do you have to be such a putz in both dimensions?"

"Why do you have to be such a doppelbitch?"

She stuck her tongue at him. "I'm on a *mission*."

He wrapped a length of twine around his collection and stuffed them into a canvas bag at his feet. "I'm only doing this because Chloe said Sere was a priority."

She wondered if this was what Dooly meant by flirting. "Don't worry, I won't let your help go to my head."

He slung his bag over his shoulder. "I've just got one question. Since you would just regenerate anyway, why was it that my dragon double didn't incinerate you when you first met? It seems like it would have been the obvious move."

"Maybe because he was nicer than you. Now, can we get going? Sere has already spent half a day in the computer. Every minute we waste is one more that Marjory Laroque has control of her body."

He let out a low growl that reminded her of his dragon double. "Come on, Midnight."

The great cat emerged from the forest and rubbed along Doodlebug's side. Bernie waited until the panther took the lead before following him into the shadows.

THE SUN BLAZED down like a demon's fiery stare. Covered in sweat, Doodlebug wondered if the hurricane-driven rains of hell were really that much of a curse compared to what the living endured. Adding to her suffering, Bernie's masculine aroma wafted behind him like the smell of a dead animal.

"You stink."

"Sorry. I might be able to duplicate the smell of sulfur from hell's brimstone if that would make you feel more at home."

She looked up at him in disgust. "Please don't."

He pointed to the dark section of trees marking Midnight's latest disappearance. "We're here."

Doodlebug pushed past Bernie and barged into the hovel. "We've got a problem."

Chloe looked up through the steam rising from her concoction brewing on the wood-burning stove. "Nice to see you too."

Doodlebug wondered why everyone in life thought they had all day for salutations and small talk. "Marjory Laroque has taken Sere's body. Sere has retreated to the professor's equipment. She believes the woman is going to abduct Sanguine in order to force her to open the hellmouth. Sere intends to go to hell, but she needs your help. Oh, and Bernie is a dick."

"I see." The swamp witch tasted her broth then set the ladle aside. "So I'm just supposed to magically let Sere's soul into hell?"

Doodlebug couldn't tell if the woman was annoyed or amused. "Something like that. I've seen you manifest your spirit in hell. Since Sere is just spirit, this can't be much different."

Chloe shook her head. "I will never understand why people think all I have to do is snap my fingers to use my magic. I can appear in hell because, as a swamp witch, I'm a part of that dimension. With the hellmouth closed, Sere would need a connection to hell that I could use to anchor her."

Doodlebug hated any explanation, be it science based or Wiccan. "Sere *is* a part of hell. Stop making my head hurt."

"Sere *was* a part of hell. Her connection was severed when Sanguine closed the door."

Midnight nudged Doodlebug in the side, nearly knocking her over in his demand for attention. She patted his massive head, wondering if all great cats were secretly little kittens inside. "I didn't think she could exist without bouncing Jennifer's image off the Cormorant in order to derive the life-sustaining power."

Chloe shrugged. "Apparently, she can—you'd have to ask the professor as to how. My point is, she's no longer tethered to hell, so there's no line for her to slide down. Even if Sanguine and I did open the gate, Sere would be just as stuck in life as she is now. To make the transition, she would need a body in hell to latch onto."

"Can we jump from your explanation of how it's impossible to where you tell me my mission?"

Chloe frowned as if Doodlebug had denied her the long-winded story that ended with the swamp witch looking brilliant for having come up with a solution. "The most obvious answer would be to enlist the Cormorant's help. She's the most direct link Sere has with hell and the only one powerful enough to pull her to the other side. Even if Sere doesn't need her energy, there should still be a connection."

Doodlebug sat on the worn afghan-covered chair. "Maybe I should have gone with the longer buildup."

Chloe poured two cups of sun tea from the large glass jar on the window shelf then handed one to Doodlebug. "The first challenge will be making contact with the deity. As you noticed, I don't have access to all of hell. I can talk to Sanguine. She may be our best opportunity to gain the Cormorant's trust, but it will still be a long shot."

"Sere isn't going to like the idea of involving the Cormorant. That birdbrain still wants Sere's body, not her soul. Even if the Cormorant did pull her into hell, it would just be in an attempt to get what she wants. Hell's self-appointed goddess couldn't give a seagull's fart about the real Marjory creating more immortals in life."

Chloe cradled the teacup in her hands and sat on the couch. "How were relations between the Cormorant and Madam Laroque when you left? Maybe we could play the enemy-of-my-enemy card."

Events had proceeded so fast in hell that Doodlebug wasn't sure who held the most chips at the end of the game. "When Smoke and I stole the vault from out of the World Trade Center, Marjory had been spying on us. After we freed Sanguine, Marjory's goons swept into the vault. Things get awfully hazy after that. Aloysius used me to complete his transformation. Sere said Sanguine got to the vault before the Cormorant could steal it back, but she lies sometimes."

Chloe sipped her tea. "Which one?"

"Which one lies?" Doodlebug frowned. "I've caught both Sere and Sanguine in stories that proved to be untrue. I can't say that's ever happened with the Cormorant."

Chloe stared into her dark brew. "And we know Marjory

can lie as easily as her bank racks up interest charges. Even with the doppelgänger edict prohibiting such acts, we have to believe Madam Laroque could spin a fib with the best of them."

Doodlebug tried the tea. The flavors of tree bark, wild herbs, and honey filled her sinuses. "What's your point?"

"The Cormorant has been lied to by everyone she's dealt with lately, and as hell's deity, she's not used to that. If I can get Sanguine to convince the Cormorant to meet me, I could gain her trust by sticking to the truth."

Again, the idea sounded incredibly bad to Doodlebug. "What would you say? Something like, 'We need you to side with us against Madam Laroque so Sere can have her body back'? That just sounds like a way of giving the Cormorant the upper hand."

Chloe grabbed some chicken bones from a bowl on a shelf then set two next to each other and a third coming in like a ship conducting a head-on attack. "Right now, Sanguine is trying to win over the Cormorant while Madam Laroque is sneaking up on them." She set a fourth bone in her empty teacup. "Sere is on the sidelines, but you can bet if the real Marjory has her way, she'll have her dimensional mirror drag Sere's soul to hell in chains."

"All while we sit drinking tea and playing with sticks." Doodlebug hated the human need to overexplain. It made things take way too long.

"Watch it, girl. I give you a lot of leeway, but we're talking about saving the world here." She pulled out the imprisoned bone and added it to the ones representing Sanguine and the

Cormorant then turned them to face Madam Laroque. "If Sere agreed to aid the Cormorant against Madam Laroque for domination of that dimension, it would be three powerful women against one. Those are far better odds than the alternative of Madam Laroque acquiring Sere's soul and holding it hostage. Our warrior will have to watch her back, but so long as there was a conflict brewing, the Cormorant wouldn't make a direct attack on Sere's soul. That would get Sere into hell to confront that version of Marjory, and it would gain us a conditional ally."

Doodlebug shrugged. As far as the fools back in the lab were concerned, she was just the messenger, not the decision maker. "What do you need from me?"

"Since Sere is stuck in the professor's computer, I can't simply manifest her to the other side. I need a direct connection to his equipment." Chloe took the two bones representing Sere and the Cormorant then added another from the bowl. "That would be the only member of the triad who's wholly in life. Even if the tether from the Cormorant to Sere is weakened, the one from Jennifer to Jenna would be as strong as ever. Hopefully, Jennifer isn't busy attending a PTA meeting, planning a dinner party, or performing some other conservative womanly duty."

"Looks like I've got another ride ahead of me." Doodlebug glared at Bernie. "Think you could find a more direct path from the cabin to the road and wait for my return somewhere I can find you?"

From his twisted face, she knew he was about to make another wildly annoying comment, but when he made eye contact with Chloe, his expression softened. "Just try to be back before dark. I'll walk you back to your motorcycle."

Chloe rounded up the bones. "While you're convincing Jennifer to risk her soul again, I'll contact Sanguine."

Doodlebug felt like a teenager asking for money. "One other thing. The motorcycle ran out of gas."

"For the love of hell." Bernie pushed open the cabin door. "I've got a truck out by the main road. We'll have to siphon off the gas."

6

———————————

*S*ere didn't remember being a disembodied nine-year-old girl in Guinee, but even though the experience didn't leave an imprint on her mind, it did on her soul. The loas of the dead disapproved of suicide. Serephine Malveaux's death, however, hadn't simply been a matter of slitting her wrists. Dark forces were at play, and that had made death's guardians sympathetic to her plight. Because of their concern, her stint in purgatory was a little like time spent in the care of her grandparents—she'd felt uncomfortable but not unwelcome.

Though the professor's computers carried none of that emotional warmth, her feeling of being in purgatory endured. The files labeled Jennifer Ellen Williams Cranston enticed Sere like a forbidden photo album of family secrets. She focused on the first entry. Young Jenny had only been eight when the professor's equipment was first powered up.

If Sere had been in a body, a lump would have formed in her throat at the image of the laughing redheaded child. Flaming locks of hair floated on the breeze as she twirled around the Moonwalk next to the river. From the metal bench, her parents kept a watchful eye on their only child but gave the girl more freedom than Sere felt appropriate. Jenny spread her arms, feeling the centrifugal force pulling at her hands. Her yellow dress spread from her hips, dipping and lifting like a merry-go-round. River birds sounded like they were laughing along with the child. If Jenny had only known how one of those blasted animals was about to be possessed by her doppelgänger spirit so Sere could take the projected body, she would not have been so carefree.

Sere closed her eyes to the memory. The projection of the happy child in hell wouldn't have had any self-awareness at the time. At least, that was the hope Sere clung to. She wondered if the Cormorant carried the same memories.

She fast-forwarded to Jenny as a preteen—tall, lanky, and uncoordinated. These were Jenny's awkward years. She'd dyed her hair blood-red in an attempt to fit in with the goth crowd. The light skin, freckles, and crystal-blue eyes, however, prevented Jenny from being accepted by anyone other than the geeky kids who sat at the back of every class.

"Who can solve this equation?" The plump woman at the front of the room had chalk dust on her forehead. Jenny had focused so much on the cosmetic faux pas that she'd missed that the woman's wandering eyes had settled on the back corner of the class.

The nerd behind Jenny intercepted the teacher's zeroing-in stare. "I can do it, Miss Arnold."

Jenny bent her head over her shoulder. "Thanks," she whispered as the boy got out of his chair.

Shit. That's Henry. Sere's shared memories of the high school nerd wouldn't fully form for another few years. Apparently, he'd been watching out for Jenny longer than she'd realized.

Curiosity got the better of Sere. She sped forward to the fateful high school football game. Jenny—now Jennifer, who'd changed her name to command the respect of the cheerleading squad—had filled out enough to attract the eye of any red-blooded high school jock. Not that it was all that difficult. She relished having broken out of her awkward phase. The budding woman's memories of boyfriends were like a dropped collection of trading cards. Faces and cocks outweighed dates and deeds. Only by turning the card over could Sere get some hint regarding how the testosterone-driven apes had treated Jennifer.

As if Sere's curiosity had somehow traveled back in time and out of the computer, Jennifer messed up her midair routine and came crashing down on her ankle. The snap seemed to fill the stadium. The rest of the squad stood, dumbstruck, fearful that the broken bone might be contagious. Even the jocks remained in their huddle. Though Sere doubted the memory was completely accurate, she couldn't help getting caught up in it.

Jennifer looked up at the stands, hoping for some authority figure to save the day. Instead, it was the nerdy kid with slicked-back hair, dorky glasses, and a bow tie who vaulted over the student body sitting in the bleachers. "Try not to move. I've got you. I'm not leaving your side."

And he never did. From that moment, Jennifer gave up jocks like an alcoholic who'd found religion—only in her case, it was lust being overwritten by love. Though no one else noticed it that day, or really any day after that, Jennifer saw the superhero under Henry's nerdy persona.

The next memory came on so fast it was like their entire courtship had happened in the blink of an eye. "Till death do us part." Jennifer held Henry's hands and gazed with tear-filled eyes into his. In his wedding tuxedo, the boy who was now a man looked as close to his superhero secret identity as Jennifer could imagine. Though still the biggest nerd she knew, he'd spent enough evenings in the gym after classes in corporate law to fill out the tux the way the designer must have intended.

Sere pulled back on the professor's projection to get a look at wedding-day Jennifer. *Good lord, woman, how long did it take to get your hair to behave?* Part of Sere's desire to keep her hair short stemmed from the never-ending need to be prepared for battle, but what she didn't want others to see was what a rats nest it would become if allowed to grow past her shoulders. Jennifer's wedding coif cascaded in waves and ringlets all the way down to her waist like a waterfall of fire. Her body displayed more curves than Sere remembered.

She backtracked to the professor's archive of projections. A solid nine months, including the wedding date, had been kept from hell's projection.

Though the calendar might have forced the decision, nothing in Jennifer's emotions betrayed anything but complete love. Jennifer hugged her new husband so tightly that the bridal gown crinkled. "I'm pregnant," she whispered in his ear.

His return hug intensified, making it hard for her to breathe. "You just had to go and make the most wonderful day of my life even better." His voice quivered so hard that Jennifer wondered if he'd be able to hold it together through the reception.

Sere felt bad for intruding on the tender moment. Though she inhabited the body double, she wasn't sure the real Jennifer would appreciate having all of her secrets divulged. *Fuck it. If it comes up, I'll just explain that when I was part of the computer, her history was automatically downloaded into my brain.*

The memory reel spun to nearly nine months later. Jennifer lay in the unbelievably undignified position of feet in the air, gown raised above her waist in the small hospital room. Far too many people were staring at her. She was screaming like a banshee. "Get this fucking parasite out of me! You're never depositing another drop of that demon sperm into my happy place again, mister." The woman gripped her husband's hand so hard his fingers crossed over each other.

Sere had no problem with swearing, but she'd always

believed her rich vocabulary stemmed from her time in hell. Jennifer's motherly love must have started sometime after delivery. At least the professor had spared Sere that experience. As she thought about it, she realized that Bobby, Jennifer's impending son, didn't have a double in hell.

The next few years unwound smoothly from the memory reel. Bobby grew into a mischievous boy who owned his mother's heart nearly as fully as her husband did. Jennifer settled into a life she had originally feared—that of suburban wife and mother. Though she still had fantasies of slaying dragons, commanding a pirate ship, and ruling over an army of devoted male warriors available for her sexual pleasure, her days of making a comfortable home for her family outweighed her lust for adventure. That was, until she learned that she had a badass devil-killing double who had inherited hell.

What surprised Sere most about the sight of Jennifer standing in the shadows outside the Scratchy Dog was how frightened she was. Fear had always been a constant companion for Sere, kind of like heartburn. So long as it was managed, it could be a useful indicator of how much trouble she'd gotten into. For Jennifer, however, the paralyzing emotion had only really made itself known when Bobby went missing. That night of absolute terror had led to the woman standing resolutely off Frenchmen Street, waiting for the apparition she didn't fully believe existed.

"Sere." The voice sounded like Jennifer.

Sere turned away from the bank of memories. "I hope someone out there has made some progress."

"I suppose that depends on your definition of progress," Doodlebug said.

Sere switched on every camera in the office but didn't see Jennifer on any of them. *"Please* tell me you aren't in hell."

"Not yet. I'm in the swamp with Chloe."

Sere checked every piece of the computer she could lock her spirit onto. "How are we communicating? That swamp witch hasn't turned you into a ghost, has she? Because one of us disconnected from her body is more than enough."

"It's called a cell phone. You should be familiar with it as it's yours," Jennifer said. As they shared the same voice, it was all too easy for Sere to make out the woman's snarky attitude. "Bart brought it out to the swamp. You weren't supposed to leave it in your saddlebags."

Sere worked at calming her nerves. "I didn't think there'd be anyone I wanted to call in Marjory's stronghold. This time spent in the professor's computer isn't doing much for my technophobia. What plan have the witches devised this time?"

"I could bore you with the specifics, but I'm not sure you'd listen. The bottom line is Chloe believes she can connect our souls over the professor's souped-up cell phone. That should get the Cormorant's attention. Once she starts pulling, Sanguine will quickly open and close the hellmouth so you can cross over. With a witch at each side of the gate, they can make sure nothing moves between dimensions that shouldn't."

Not this again. Sere had already struggled to get Jennifer out of hell once. "I'm going to stop you right there. I need to go alone."

"And do what?" Bart's husky voice blared over the connection. "You'll still be stuck in the computer. You don't have a body, and I don't see your father around to steal you another one. You and Jennifer have already proved that one of you can act as bodily anchor while the other tags along as a ghost."

She suspected he was intentionally drawing her anger so Jennifer wouldn't receive her demon glare. "That's a low blow, mister."

"I'm just saying, even if Sanguine could get you out of the hardware, you'd just be a ghost in hell, destined to evaporate into nothingness."

Even if Sere hadn't just witnessed a lifetime of memories that bonded her to her real more than she thought possible, she still wouldn't have allowed Jennifer to risk her soul a second time. Jennifer didn't always see it, but Henry and Bobby relied on her completely. "Tell Chloe she and Sanguine need to figure out something else, because if it comes down to my immortal existence or Jennifer's soul, I'm out."

"You can be the most pigheaded doppelidiot ever released from hell," Jennifer yelled. "I have a say in my own life, you know. It's not just your *precious* existence either. You may not have that much invested in the living, but I do. If you think I'm going to sit by while hell takes over the world that Bobby is going to have to live in, you've lost your fucking doppelbrain."

From the cameras in the professor's office, Sere could

see that not a single person moved toward the microphone. They remained as silent as the people on the other end of the cell connection. "Good thing you never chastised Bobby about using such language. Hell wouldn't be much fun devoid of curse words." Sere hadn't meant to express the thought, but the computer wasn't much good at understanding when she wanted to keep her words to herself.

Doodlebug gave a girlish laugh that failed to cut the tension. "Now that you've all shut your faces for a moment, maybe I can offer some advice. After all, I am the only one who's been a ghost in the professor's hell hardware, and I've seen Aloysius's soul get yanked out of the equipment."

"That was different," Sere said. "You still had your doppelgänger body. As for your time in the hardware, it was as part of Marjory's bridge of the damned. You weren't stuck there like I would be. Not that it matters. Following Chloe's recommendation would mean dropping Jennifer in hell without either of us physically there to protect her. You've seen her. She's no warrior."

"Hey, I'm on your side on this one," the girl said. "I was there. Neither one of you would have gotten out without my help. I'm just saying, when it comes to figuring something out, I do have some experience in these things."

"How about this," Jennifer said. "So long as you and I aren't physically and psychically bonded, the Cormorant can't pull me into hell unless I agree to go. She'll sense that we're together, but with you in the computer, when she pulls on the line, you'll just slip right across. This way, I'll be here to reel you back in when the time comes."

Sere finally found the phone's connection to the lab and activated the camera. Chloe sat in her chair with Midnight at her side—Doodlebug on the floor, petting the great cat at Chloe's feet—while Bart paced the half dozen steps from one side of the hovel to the other. Only Jennifer remained focused on the phone.

"I can see you've thought this through. Have you all been planning this attack?" Sere asked.

Bart stopped his pacing. "Like it or not, you need our help. Simply having Sanguine open the portal won't allow you to slip into hell, and once you're there, you're going to need to do more than just haunt our enemies."

Sere eased back into the computer software. "Okay. So the first job—which I do not like but have to agree with—is Jennifer connects to me while Sanguine opens the gate."

Bart took his hand from his chin. "What do you need? What's the plan for when you're in hell?"

"I need to get to Madam Laroque. She's the only one our Marjory in life can rely on."

He nodded as he put his hands in his back pockets. "The Cormorant is the only power in hell that can rival Madam Laroque. With any luck, Sanguine can play middle angel in that negotiation. But you still won't have a body. That's the real issue, isn't it?"

"Doesn't Sanguine have the baron's old vault?" Doodlebug asked.

Bart aimed his finger at the girl. "True. She might be able to put Sere into another body the way the baron did so many years ago, but we don't have his journals, and with the doppelgängers achieving consciousness, we can't see them as vacant vessels."

"Even if it was only temporary?" Polly sat next to the professor in the lab, doodling her thoughts on the ever-present pad of paper.

"Too many complications," the professor said. "We'd need the doppelgänger's acceptance, and even then, we don't know how to make the transfer—unless someone wants to break into the bank and steal the baron's old journals."

"We don't have to." Sere turned her attention away from the computers. "Marjory is inside my body. I can't force her to do anything, but I can put the seeds of doubt in *my* brain. That might be enough for her to rummage through the journals again just for peace of mind."

"One problem down," Bart said. "Now, about that body."

Doodlebug bit her lip as she turned to Chloe. "Where's Bernie?"

"Now you're talking." The swamp witch kicked the great cat off her feet. "Go find Bernie, Midnight, and be quick about it." Chloe headed to the door. The moment she opened it, the panther darted outside and was lost to the moonlight shadows.

Doodlebug seemed to have trouble looking into the phone. "I'd offer to go with you—"

Sere didn't need the half-hearted offer. "You're out of hell. That was our agreement. I may have a human soul, but I've lived the doppelgänger life for too long to play games with the truth. If you were to return to hell, I couldn't guarantee that you could leave again. I'm not asking anyone to risk their existence on my behalf—not again."

~

"I'M COMING WITH YOU." Bart's cold analytical tone as he held the cell phone to his face didn't leave room for argument.

Sere had anticipated his demand, though she feared her argument might sound more emotional than logical. "Even if I agreed, which I do not, I need you here in life as my lifeline. You know that."

"Nice try." He kept his voice down as if unsure he wanted the others to hear. "Jennifer just offered to risk everything she is to help you, and you just protected her like a mother lion. She said she can act as your connection to this reality, and if for some reason that doesn't work, I can come back through the hellmouth first then pull your soul across."

"How do you expect this is going to work? I barely understand how I'm making it to hell and back."

"I'm going to send a message to Sanguine via Chloe. Once the hellmouth is open, I'm riding Lefty through the gate. If it worked for doppelgängers escaping hell, I don't see why it wouldn't work for a human entering that dimension. After all, Agnes originally designed the portal to get her plants and animals across."

Fuck, Sere thought. The sight of his magnificently buff body sometimes made her forget that he had an equally impressive brain. "They won't go along with it."

"I can be pretty convincing when I get my charm on. The way I see it, Sanguine is going to have her hands full. She needs to find a voodoo totem then transfer you into it from the professor's hell-based computer. After that, she'll need to snag the doppelgänger Smoke in his human shape. He's not going to fit in the vault in his dragon form, so Sanguine will have to fly both of you out to the swamp island. Assuming all goes well, which it almost never does, she'll then be in charge of making the transfer."

Though he did a fine job of laying out the plan, Sere didn't see why he felt the need to risk his life and soul to hell's dimension. "And where do you see yourself being needed?"

"Security. If Madam Laroque gets even one whiff that the gate is open, she'll be sending every available demon she can round up out to the swamp. Then there's the Cormorant to consider."

Sere was happy to be disembodied at the moment. She wouldn't have wanted him to see her defeat. "You don't trust her?"

"Do you?" His question cut her to the circuit board.

"No. Though she wants my body and can't have it while Marjory is in possession of it, that doesn't mean she won't try—especially with me already out of it." Attempting to take back command of the expedition while still conceding that Bart had a point, Sere said, "Fine. I need your help. Ask Doodlebug who she trusted in hell. Though I don't want to risk the living, we're going to need every doppelgänger we can rely on."

"I'm on it. It's going to be strange seeing you as a dude, or worse, a dragon."

Though she'd never admit it out loud, the thought of having him at her side brought a flutter to whatever passed for her heart in the computer. "Just don't go getting any ideas that because I'm not in a human form, you can order me around. And thanks."

"I did warn you that I wouldn't let you rot in hell without me."

7

*S*ere regained consciousness inside the all-too-familiar iron vault. "I swear, this place still smells like my father."

"Pipe smoker, was he?"

She put her hand to the stubbled chin. Both comments had come from the masculine voice, like two people walking through a revolving door. She wasn't alone. "Thanks for the use of your body. I know how big a deal this is."

"Hey, I get to live my life as a dragon. I always knew that shifter ability came with unspecified obligations. A word of advice on becoming the dragon: I find it's easiest not to focus too much on the transformation. It can be pretty disorienting. Speaking of which, you'd better get moving. Feels like Bernie just took a shot of dragon's breath. I'll be hanging here out in the totem when you're done."

Sere pushed against the door, momentarily surprised

that the heavier masculine body could move the heavy iron hatch so easily. The hinges screeched as it opened far enough for her to fall out and land on the ground. Her head pounded like railroad tracks under a freight train. She squeezed her eyes closed against the sensation of hot daggers being plunged into them.

"We need to get her away from the vault." Bart's words rang out through the din in her mind.

Hands grabbed her around the arms, legs, and torso. She couldn't tell how many, but there were more than just the two that belonged to Bart. The ground rasped against her back as if she were too heavy to be lifted completely. They dropped her on her belly.

The barrage of sensations finally overloaded the doppelgänger brain. Everything went silent and dark. Even her arms and legs seemed like distant memories. A breeze that should have ruffled her hair played around her head and neck.

She opened her eyes. Treetops spread out like the pile of a thick carpet all the way to the surrounding hurricane. Sere shook her head in an attempt to make sense of the inputs that didn't match up.

In front of one of her eyes, Sanguine hovered like Tinker Bell. "Keep your eye on me." She flew forward.

Sere focused on the swamp fairy until she disappeared directly in front of her nose then reappeared before Sere's other eye. Sanguine spread her hands wide and returned to a spot directly in front of Sere, who could see one hand with each eye but not the woman herself.

"There's a blind spot directly in front of you. When you spit fire, this is where you'll be hitting."

Sere nodded. "Okay."

"Feel like joining the conversation?"

Sere looked down. Forty feet below her, Bart stood next to Lefty, looking like a little boy with his overly large dog. She eased her limbs into bent positions until she felt the grass-covered ground sink under her as if she was lying down on a mattress. Then she put her head on the ground. For the first time in her life, Lefty looked like a little lizard. "This is all so strange."

Sanguine lighted next to Bart. "We've got work to do. I set up a meeting with the Cormorant. I should warn you that I did have to disclose that it's *you* in the dragon body."

Back in life, Sere would have considered the betrayal unforgivable. In hell, brutal honesty was the only approach that would make the Cormorant agree to the meeting. "Did she offer any assurances that she wouldn't try to abduct my soul in exchange for my body?"

Sanguine folded her arms over her stomach. "She agreed to the meeting. All things considered, I took that as a victory. She doesn't trust me very much. For what it's worth, Smoke made quick work of the Cormorant's flying contingent, so you've got that power on your side if things turn ugly."

Sere looked past Lefty to where the vault had been, feeling bad about asking so much from that side of Chloe's apprentice. "I guess with Smoke inside the totem and vault and back between dimensions, he's about as safe as we can make him." She turned her giant dragon eye to Bart. "And what's your plan?"

"I thought I might bum a ride from you into the city. Doodlebug left me a list of her street-warrior contacts. No matter how your chat goes with your weird-ass Jennifer-mirror deity, we're eventually going to have to confront whatever army Madam Laroque has drummed up."

Sere looked back toward her gator lounging in the weeds. "You'd better stay here, boy. Even with the vault being invisible, I can't risk either of those hell powers trying to do an end run on me."

His snort leveled the grass for ten feet in front of him.

SERE FOUND FLYING to be remarkably easy. Even with Bart on her back, a couple of swings of the giant dragon wings lifted her clear of the trees.

Sanguine flew beside her like a pilot boat directing a cargo ship upriver. "Stretch your wings out a little farther, and you won't have to beat them so often."

Yes, Mom. Other than from Joe Cazenave, Sere never had been able to take instruction without it setting off her snarky attitude, and the only reason she accepted guidance from the former Army Ranger was because he'd drop her on her ass if she gave him any back talk. She figured that trying another of the body's special powers—one that Sanguine didn't share—might get the angel off her back. "I'm dropping down to treetop level. I want to test out the flame-throwing ability."

Sanguine flapped her gossamer-white wings a little harder. "I think I'll stay up here."

Sere spread her wings as far as they would go and angled her head down like the fiery flying serpent from hell that she'd heard about in stories. "Hang on, Bart." She puffed up her chest then blew the air out of her nostrils. All that came out was snot, which covered the tops of the cypress and oak trees. "That didn't work."

Bart lay against the back of her neck. His head rested so close behind her ear that she flapped it in irritation. "Maybe you have to be mad, the way you get when you go all demonic."

"That would make sense. Say something that you know will make me angry."

"Why do I have to do everything? It's like every problem you encounter, you just figure I'll come sailing in to your rescue. For a badass demon-hunting daughter of the devil, you can be a real prima donna at times."

She gritted her teeth and blew out her lungs so she could fully refill them for an irate response. The puff of air she let out, however, set the oak below her ablaze. "You did that intentionally."

His laugh further fueled her irritation. "You told me to make you mad."

She focused her anger through her nose. As Sanguine had explained, she didn't see the main body of fire, only the way it lit up the sky in front of her and created a bonfire below. "At least we figured out how to activate the flames."

She felt him squirming around on her back. Even without seeing what he was doing, she could feel his tensed-muscle call to action that accompanied the drawing of weapons. "If you're done playing," he said, "it looks like someone sent us a welcome party. Straight ahead and a tick above us."

She angled her head to see the flock of oversized bat-like baby dragons. "Must be from Marjory. It would appear that back in life, she's still abducting druggies for her little experiment, or these were leftovers from her invasion force. You don't suppose they followed Sanguine and Smoke out here, do you?"

"That, or they're the remnants from the group that attacked Doodlebug. They could have just been hanging out, waiting to see what emerged from the hellmouth. Still, I would have thought they'd hightail it back to their mistress with their report rather than engage in combat."

"Let's make sure they don't get the chance." Sere beat her wings to get above the squadron.

Sanguine had her gleaming silver sword drawn. "They may be small, stoned, and stupid, but even children with matches can set things on fire."

Sere didn't like the flammable look of Sanguine's feathered wings. "Let me take first crack at them." She folded in her wings before the angel had time to argue.

The little flaming fuckers came up at her from the treetops like mosquitoes out of the grass. Without being able to see straight ahead, Sere let out a blast of fire, hoping some were stupid enough to be directly ahead.

A loud explosion from her back made her swing wildly away from the flock. "What the hell was that?"

Bart was busy doing something between her shoulders.

"I exchanged weapons with Doodlebug. She left me her flintlock. She thought it might be useful here. I've gotta say, this thing packs a punch. Did you see that little flamehead tumble out of the sky?"

"I can't see anything other than what's coming up alongside of me, like that breakaway contingent overhead."

"Swing your head side-to-side while you're discharging the fire. Slash your flame like it's a sword. That's the way they do it in the movies." He settled back into place. "I've got a shot ready and my knives within easy reach."

She had no intention of letting the little flintheads get near enough for Bart to need his blades. A little dragon missing half a wing tumbled beside her. Looking up, Sere noticed that Sanguine's sword was dripping with blood. "Those little fuckers are everywhere."

"They're gathering above us," Bart said. "Sanguine's doing what she can, but we need to take a more commanding vantage point."

Sere could imagine Joe telling her the same thing in a tone of controlled irritation. Any time she'd truly been in trouble, he'd resorted to curt commands rather than yelling. With half a dozen good strokes of her wings, she was well above the action. A dozen little dragons were rotating their attack on Sanguine. Each came away with more damage than victory, but the angel was seriously outnumbered.

"Dive for the riverbank, Sanguine," Sere said. The angel needed the extra protection of the woods, and even if the little monsters could sail after her between the trees, they couldn't outfly the big dragon.

As the angel folded her wings and made her escape, Sere

dove snout first through the cloud of black dragons. With flames erupting from her nostrils like bug spray discharged into a swarm of cockroaches, Sere disbanded Marjory's latest contingent of flying lizards. The ones that didn't fall to the trees with wings on fire screeched in fear as they headed in every direction away from the great swamp dragon.

"We can't let them escape," Bart yelled.

They were already at the edge of the hurricane. "Well, I can't go flying off in every direction!"

Sanguine glided down beside Sere. "It won't matter. It's not like Smoke hasn't been seen before. Even if her little spies didn't see us playing around with the vault, the fact that you're back in hell isn't a secret we'll be able to keep for long. Our best bet now is to meet with the Cormorant."

"And the sooner the better," Sere said. "If Marjory intends on plopping out dragons, we'll be inundated with the little bastards."

8

Though Sere had been out of hell—and the eternally midnight hurricane—for over a year, some experiences came back as easily as putting on a moldy old coat. The hurricane wasn't as daunting as it had been in the past. In the dragon body, she finally had the means of combating the storm. "Flying this thing isn't half-bad."

Bart remained safely behind the flap of her ear. "Speak for yourself." He pointed toward the freeway just beyond the airport. "Set me down just past the Kenner exit. Doodlebug said she has spies staked out there just in case Marjory got any bright ideas about sending demons on foot back to the hellmouth."

Sere nodded, undulating the reptilian neck more than she'd intended and causing Bart to hang on tighter. "Any thoughts on how we'll stay in contact?" She set her clawed feet on the off-ramp and arched her back so he could slide off.

He worked around in front of her, her body shielding him from the wind. "Well, we don't dare use any connections involving the professor's lab. We can't risk either Marjory or the Cormorant getting their hands on the tether to your soul."

A shudder went along her back all the way down her tail. "And Chloe is too far away to be a useful intermediary."

"Doodlebug said she used to leave a journal in the cemetery so she could communicate with Dooly."

Sere spread her wings in frustration. "Do I look like I could operate a pen?"

"No, but my point was that the cemetery is as close to neutral ground as we're going to find in hell."

Sere snorted out a small flame that she angled away from him. "I can get there without any problem, but you're going to be a little limited in getting around on those flooded streets."

He jingled a set of keys in front of her. "Doodlebug also told me where to find Joe's souped-up motorcycle. Do what you've gotta do with the Cormorant. I'll round up as many doppelgängers as I can. Then we'll regroup at the cemetery. I doubt anyone is going to expect us to return to the scene of your bodily abduction."

Though she admired his ability to adjust to any environment, his inherent inclination to command could be his undoing in a dimension where he didn't know the rules and players. A region filled with harvesters on the hunt was no place for a human. "Just remember, you're in hell, and these demons you'll be dealing with aren't the same as humans."

He gave her the half-snarky, half-charming smile that cut through her emotional defenses. "I do have some experience dealing with a resident of hell."

She felt a little stupid blushing as a dragon. "Just because you won me over doesn't mean Doodlebug's warriors are going to follow you."

"I understand mercenaries even better than women. If I don't show up with a dozen skilled soldiers, feel free to say, 'I told you so.'"

"Don't think I won't." It was as close to a plan as Sere could hope for. She looked out at the storm circling the city. "I should be done first, so I'll be able to clear the grounds of any stray goblins. I can't tell you to be careful. This is hell, and you'll have to put it all on the line to survive."

His eyes still held the love she remembered. "I'll meet you at the cemetery."

THE HALF-DESTROYED warehouse on the river gave Sere the chills. The last time she was in the open-sided beam structure, she'd been hauling Jennifer's soul toward the professor's lab while avoiding the very being she was now trying to meet. "Did we have to have our talk here?" She kept her neck bent to avoid hitting her scaly head against the corrugated metal roof.

Sanguine ruffled the rain out of her feathers. "It was the only place big enough to accommodate you as a dragon. With the open sides, the three of us could fly in from any direction—or out if things go wrong."

A flock of birds glided in along the riverside then set up a perimeter. The Cormorant landed within it. The birdwoman stood straight as if trying to command the stage, but at seven feet tall, she looked like a little stuffed mama bird behind her flock of chicks from Sere's vantage point. "So we finally meet." The Cormorant flexed her fist, rippling a small scar on her arm.

Sere got a flash of memory from when the Cormorant had swooped in and cut Jennifer's arm with her beak. "We can discuss our issues another time. Our mutual enemy is about to make a move on the living."

"Why should I care?" Her squawking voice hurt Sere's reptilian ears.

She tried to control her breath to avoid filling the cavernous space with fire. "I'm not stupid. I know you're fighting her doppelgänger for control over hell. Let me help you." She spread her wings, nearly touching the side support beams. "Her dragons are no match for me."

The Cormorant folded her arms behind her wings. "And in exchange, I suppose you want me to abandon my quest for *my* original body?"

Sere never could figure out why Jenna was so fixated on being a human-shaped doppelgänger. "If all I cared about was staying out of your talons, I'd have remained in life."

The birdwoman turned her blazing black eyes on Sere. "I'm not stupid either. You wouldn't be in that dragon if you still had control of your body. Maybe I should side with Marjory Laroque. I'll bet she'd be more than happy to give me that scrawny-ass female form in exchange for freeing her from your meddling."

Sere wondered if that had been Marjory's long game. "I'm sure she would, but then you'd be under her command. Think about it, Jenna. As a birdwoman, you're a deity in hell. As a normal doppelgänger, you'd have no claim."

Not a feather moved on the Cormorant. "Never use that name again."

Sanguine moved between the two and spread her wings as if signaling the end of round one. "This isn't getting us anywhere. Sere isn't turning loose of her body, but her help isn't contingent on you giving up your quest. For now, put your differences aside so we can focus on our shared enemy. Where are you at with establishing peace between the harvesters and doppelgängers?"

The Cormorant shrugged her wings and pointed her beak at Sere. "About as well as you're doing with me and my body snatcher over there."

Sanguine put her hands on her hips while keeping her wings spread wide. It was a stance Sere remembered well. "Are you finished?"

The Cormorant lowered her wings. "The harvesters obey my commands, but many of the doppelgängers still believe they can have safety by taking one of Madam Laroque's coins."

Sere had gotten enough of a rundown from Doodlebug to realize how misguided the attempted union had been between the powerful women. "Isn't it your face on the other side of the doubloon?"

Sanguine looked over her shoulder and glared at Sere. "This squabbling isn't helping."

Sere lowered her head. "I was just pointing out that as

the Cormorant, she does bear some responsibility for so many doppelgängers missing limbs."

Sanguine lowered her wings so far that the tips touched the wet concrete floor. "This is pointless. You two are never going to agree to anything."

"We both hate Marjory Laroque." The Cormorant aimed the comment up at Sere. "That's something at least. I'm not working with you. That would involve a level of trust we'll never achieve, but I also won't stand against you. Though Madam Laroque might be able to work with her real to get me my body, she has an annoying way of dangling the carrot without ever delivering the prize. I'd rather take my chances on my own. Just don't cross me or go after my harvesters the way your minion did."

"So you'd leave me to do your dirty work?" Sere asked.

"Girls!" Sanguine's wings shook, quivering every single feather.

Sere's snicker was quickly followed by the Cormorant's chirping. One of them was a dragon and the other a seven-foot-tall birdwoman—*girl* didn't really fit either of them.

Sanguine said, "I swear to my grandmother, if one of you makes one more snarky comment, I'm out of here."

Sere knew she'd pushed her angel farther than she should have. She lowered her head to the Cormorant's level. "Can you tell me what I'll be up against? With you commanding the harvesters and the doppelgänger loyalty in disarray, who is Marjory using for her army?"

She could practically see the irritating response forming on the Cormorant's face. With a glance at the irate angel, however, the Cormorant's expression softened. "You already know about her idiot dragons. No offense."

"None taken. Chloe used a different brand of magic—as well as source material—in creating this form."

The Cormorant nodded. "Well, since her dragons were something of a disappointment, she moved on to other goblins. There's a pack of wild half-sentient dogmen that patrol the cemetery walls."

Shit. Sere hoped Bart was taking his time finding doppelgänger allies and not doing something foolish like trying to beat her to the cemetery. "I think our business is finished here. If we never see each other again, that would be just fine by me." She turned and took flight before Sanguine could throw another glare of pseudo-parental disdain at her.

MUCH AS SERE enjoyed riding motorcycles, she had to admit that flying as a dragon was pretty fucking cool. She just wished she could have a moment to enjoy the ride without it being a mad rush into battle. She sailed low over the French Quarter. If the doppelidiots were easily swayed by the promises of someone adept at lying, perhaps their loyalty to Madam Laroque did not run very deep. The sight of a dragon who dwarfed Madam Laroque's little windup toys just might make them switch to Sere's side. As she flew toward Rampart Street, she could feel the flames boiling in her stomach. Before she let her anger loose, however, she needed to make sure Bart wasn't in the line of fire.

At the old brick wall that surrounded the cemetery, she spread her wings and made a quick circle of the grounds. Though she didn't see the motorcycle, that didn't mean he hadn't stashed it somewhere out of sight. She glided as low as she dared to peek into every open door and hidden alley. Convinced that he wasn't within firing range, she got ready to flap her wings to a commanding position.

The ravenous pack of doppeldogs launched out of the tenement windows and onto Sere's back. Individually, they wouldn't have been able to drag her down, but as paws pounded against her wings and ravenous teeth tried to penetrate her scales, she lost her command of the air. Before she could land into the sharp claws and razor fangs, she grabbed the cemetery wall and propelled her body away from the buildings filled with Marjory's goblin hounds. She tumbled against the tombs, knocking the demon dogs from her back and delivering a scorching reminder of her dragon ability to their tails. From out of the crypts, dark figures in black hoods emerged all around her. She took in a deep breath to deliver another fiery response to the harvesters.

"We're on your side," the leader yelled. "Bart sent us. We're part of Doodlebug's army." The doppelgänger shed the stolen black cape.

"Get these mongrels off my back!" Sere yelled.

The doppelgängers lunged off the tops of the tombs like ninjas, tumbled along the streets of the dead, and swung swords at the hairy beasts. Other than swatting the bad dogs with her talons, there wasn't much Sere could do to help.

From above, Marjory's second wave descended. The small dragons dove and banked among the marble structures with the skills of swallows. With Bart's warriors so close, Sere didn't dare bust loose and fill the cemetery with flames. The little bastards, on the other hand, had figured out how to use their hand-torch-sized fires with pinpoint accuracy. Trapped between the goblin hounds and the dragons, the doppelgänger army was forced to retreat toward the back of the cemetery.

"Oh, hell, no." Sere sent an arching blast of fire overhead then took to the sky. She wasn't about to let Bart's hard work of rounding up recruits get pissed away by a mangy pack of dogs and amped-up fireflies. She made a quick dragon-swatting bank turn that tossed the little flamers toward the front gate.

"Keep watch overhead, Sere. Help has arrived."

She swung her head around. Bart stood in front of a contingent easily twice the size of the advanced force that had come to her aid. They seemed to have manifested right out of the tombs. If she was going to maintain the advantage, she couldn't take time to question the source of the reinforcements. With two hard flaps of her wings, she sailed over the enemy force while sending a blistering fire down on them. As she passed, Bart's second wave moved in. The demonic dogs scrambled for the front gate. Faced with failure, the once-organized pack deteriorated into every mutt for himself. The small dragons attempted an escape by flying over the advancing mercenaries. Sere waited until they were a good twenty feet above the ground before filling the sky with her fiery rage.

∼

WITH MARJORY'S creatures skulking away—their scaly and fluffy tails between their legs—Sere landed on top of a mausoleum. She peered into the open tombs. "How many friggin' doppelgängers did you cram into those crypts? You guys were like clowns coming out of a tiny car."

Bart wiped the blood from his blades on the pelt of a downed hound. "It occurred to me that though the living Marjory Laroque has unlimited funds for purchasing property, the hell version of the woman has to live by the laws of this dimension."

Sere shook her head. Bart could get a little full of himself after a victory. "What are you talking about?"

He waved his swords around the cemetery. "Doppelgängers are based on the professor's equipment, but the structure of hell comes from Agnes Delarosa. The basic elements of the properties don't change."

Sere was beginning to follow his reasoning. "So the tunnel under the French Quarter couldn't be sealed off from the other buildings."

"Exactly. Back in life, we busted into the bank's basement by using the tunnel. That's what alerted our Marjory to the weakness in her defenses. Since neither of us has a duplicate in hell, and Madam Laroque is nearly as independent as her real, there was no reason why she would have known about the tunnel. And even if she had, all she could do was position guards. Since she seemed to be going through soldiers at an alarming rate, I assumed she didn't have any spare ones to sit around a dark hole, waiting for intruders. I used the same basement we crawled through in life to access the tunnel. From there, it was just a matter of racing down it to the first rotting casket we came to. The ancestor pits under the Laroque mausoleums run deep."

Bart's smarts never failed to impress her. "Since we'd agreed to meet at the cemetery, you figured there might be an ambush. That's why you sent the advanced force."

"We knew Marjory was using the druggies around the cemetery for her experiments. I wasn't sure she'd have a force waiting for us, but since some of the dragons escaped us out in the swamp, it was a good bet she knew something was up." A good two dozen doppelwarriors stood at attention behind Bart.

"Forgive me for ever doubting your abilities."

He sheathed his swords. "This isn't the first strange place I've landed in without support. Being dropped off in an enemy's home turf with nothing but my wits and rounding up a paramilitary force with little resources was my specialty."

"You sound like Joe."

He ignored the compliment. "How did it go with the Cormorant?"

"Horrible. She says she'll stay out of our way while we deal with her enemy, but that's all I got out of her."

"That's big of her. Where do you want to start?"

Sere struggled to keep the pieces of the puzzle in front of her. "I need Marjory out of my body—or as Jenna would say, *her* body—but that's kind of the final step before we return to the living. Those demons and dragons she hauled into life are the ones that worry me. But even if we can't end her new devil, if we cut her pets' cords that pass through hell, the creatures should dissipate."

Bart paced in front of his band of doppelmercenaries. "Each of them has both the real and double in life, so what's left in hell to cut?"

"Dammit, how could I be so stupid?" Sere dug her talons into the marble roof, crumbling the stone to dust.

He stopped pacing. "What are you thinking?"

"She doesn't have a computer, but she does have access to the voodoo totems that were left in the restaurant on top of the World Trade Center."

Bart rubbed his chin. "There were only eight of them."

"That's still a lot of dragons in life. I have to talk to Sanguine. She must have found a spare to transport my soul out to the swamp. Where there's one, there may be more. I've been so focused on the professor's equipment and the Wiccan realm that I completely ignored the voodoo component of hell. I guess I assumed with Baron Samedi on our side, maybe I'd get a pass. That was stupid."

"Don't beat yourself up over it. Kendell and Myles bear more than a little responsibility for that side of hell. Would those totems be able to act as mirrors?"

"I don't see why not. If a soul can get locked in one the way Sanguine did to transfer me from the computer to the swamp, it shouldn't be that hard to cast a spell into the spirit jar. Dammit, I've even seen Chloe do something similar with her fucking mirror jars."

"Okay. At least now we know what we're looking for. Do you think Madam Laroque would hide them in the bank basement?"

Sere flapped her wings to remove the self-recrimination. "No. According to Doodlebug, Marjory has the real models for her monsters locked in her mansion in life. It would make sense to have the mirrors stashed in the same basement in hell."

He looked up and down her reptilian body without saying a word.

She spread her wings. "Not very stealthy, am I?" Fitting into a basement, even if it wasn't underground, would be impossible.

"I'm always looking for the advantages. I've got a pretty decent mercenary force. Since it seems unlikely that there will be another grand ball in the mansion like the one Doodlebug attended, our incursion will need a distraction."

"That's a relief. For a second, I thought you were going to suggest I transform into Bernie's body."

"Our situation is dicey enough without you experimenting with Chloe's cocktails. Once we're inside and have the totems, what do we do with them?"

Sere's first instinct was to chop the wooden heads into kindling, but messing with voodoo without knowing what she was doing had a bad way of biting her in the ass. "I'll need to check with Kendell. Hopefully, it's just a matter of smashing the blue-glass jars, but I wouldn't want you turning curses and spells loose while you and your mercenaries were trapped in the room."

"So we need Sanguine. Any idea where she ended up after your meeting?"

Sere wasn't in a hurry to confront her angel again. The woman was pretty pissed after the failed negotiations. "She's probably working on calming the Cormorant." She hated to admit it, but a distraction would be a whole lot easier if they had the big bird's help.

"So long as you're making contact with the other side, if Fisher can work his magic, I could use the blueprints to the Laroque mansion. While you're having your chat, I'll take my army and scout things out."

She was grateful for the change of topic. "He probably already has them in his desk. At some point, he stopped waiting for me to ask for information and started compiling as much data on our adversaries as he could find."

"Does every superhero have a sidekick with a magical desk drawer where all of the answers reside?"

"Well, this one does." Laughing made fire spurt out of her snout. "It would probably be best if we didn't rendezvous here again."

"That hidden cache of Joe's in the Ninth Ward seems pretty secluded."

The memory of their first time having sex made her wish she didn't have to deal with the dragon body. "I remember it well." The purring that emanated from deep in her chest sent a tendril of smoke up from her nostrils.

"Yeah, you were smoking hot that day too."

She sighed out a wavering candle-sized flame. "I only wish it were in the same way. I'll carry the memory of that first night together until the day I die. Which may mean your sexual prowess will be immortalized forever."

"I'll take a rain check on trying to equal the performance. When we get back to our lives, we may need a week in bed."

She feared that if the conversation continued, she'd be

setting the cemetery alight with more than a dim glow. Being in the dragon body, with an army of mercenary doppelgängers standing at attention, probably wasn't the most romantic of settings. "I'll meet you at the shack as soon as I'm done with Kendell."

Though Sere didn't believe in goodbyes, she desperately wanted to kiss him. *Probably just as well that I can't.*

9

*S*ere glided over the river, keeping an eye out for the white angel riding the wind. Though Sanguine would have her hands full dealing with Jenna, Sere doubted the pair had remained together for long after her departure. The angel was slow to anger, but once aroused, she often needed time and space to cool down. Though Sanguine never admitted to it, Sere suspected she used the flights to peek on future events. If that were the case, the woman would know Sere was searching for her.

Out over the swamp, Sere glimpsed a flash of white wings. She banked away from the city, grateful to not have to face the Cormorant or her squadron of squawking gulls. The dragon body easily curved through the wind like it was being called home.

Sanguine landed on a grassy field. The large water-filled dragon prints suggested that the area was well known to

Smoke. Sere glided to a raised hump of ground and set her feet on relatively dry land.

Chloe emerged from the trees, flanked by Doodlebug and Jennifer. "How can we help?" the swamp witch asked Sanguine.

The white angel turned to Sere. "Ask her. I'm just the guide this time."

Sere wanted to probe Sanguine on what she saw in the future, but the angel would just give her the standard line that telling someone about what was to come invariably changed what was meant to be. She guessed that was also how the swamp witch found an additional voodoo totem just lying around unused. Chloe's dimensional projection of the trio in life made them look like ghosts in the storm. "Bart needs Fisher to dig up the drawings for the Laroque mansion. I'm pretty sure there are voodoo totems in this dimension's basement that mirror Marjory's druggies through hell to their dragon doubles. I need Kendell to figure out how to destroy the wooden heads to break the connection."

"Sounds like you've been a busy girl." Chloe pulled a phone from her dress. "Anyone else I should conference in?"

"That depends. How are things going in life?" Though Sere remained focused on her hell adventure, that didn't mean Marjory was just sitting on Sere's ass. The woman had to be up to something.

"According to Kendell's spies among the homeless population, more than a few members of the Laroque family failed to show up to work."

Sere wondered where the woman was stashing her

relatives. She doubted they were hanging out in either basement with the other monsters or druggies. "If Marjory thinks she has all the pieces, she's going to start experimenting with building her toys."

Sanguine held her wings over her head to keep the rain off of her. "She still doesn't have access to the professor's computer. Even if she does manage to combine human and doppelgänger, they won't be immortal without the data needed to regenerate. The doppelenergy from those dragons of hers will be sucked dry with the demons' first skirmish."

Sere had forgotten how helpful Sanguine could be in seeing the bigger picture. "That would explain why she's been staying out of sight. She doesn't want to start a war until she's ready."

Chloe started punching the phone's screen. "I've texted your questions to those involved. I'm also calling in Polly and the professor. They've got some questions about what Marjory is up to with your body."

Sere wanted to tell her to stop, but the truth was that she was a little curious herself. "I doubt I know much more than they do, but our talks do occasionally kick things loose that I hadn't considered." While Chloe dabbled with her screen, Sere turned to Doodlebug. "What did you find out on your tour of the Northshore?"

With arms crossed and feet spread, the girl looked ready for a fight. "No one's seen Aloysius, though I still believe he didn't go through the vault system."

"Trust your feelings. I know that's not natural coming from hell," Sere said. If she and Bart were going to conduct their operation, someone would need to distract Marjory, and only Doodlebug had experience facing down demons. "How are you set for doing battle?"

"Even if I could get at the demons, I can't go up against a horde of hell's creatures on my own."

The girl was going to need help, and Sere was running short of allies she could trust in either dimension. "Get on your motorcycle and ride north. About ten miles before you hit Bart's bar, you'll run into a dirt parking lot and a shack called Riley's. The woman has tried to kill me more than once."

"I like her already," Doodlebug grumbled.

"My point being, she's not afraid of going up against doppelgängers, and her customers can be a rough bunch. They don't like me, but they do owe me a favor. If you can't find enough help among the gator hunters, continue up to Bart's. The bikers up there are more talk than fight, but not a one of them would let their favorite bartender rot in hell. Your first priority is still to find Aloysius. He's the only confirmed devil at this point." Sere wished she could point the girl toward Gerald, but as he was the devil's grandfather, she didn't dare test his loyalties until she could do so in person. "Just locate Aloysius—don't go up against him."

The girl lowered her head and clenched her fists. "I'm not stupid. I have no intention of confronting that bastard until you're back here and we're at full force. He's already ripped my spirit to pieces once."

Sere nodded. "Knowing where he is and what he's up to will help when it's finally time to confront him. Marjory's other creations, however, are fair game should you run across them. That will at least give you an outlet for your aggression."

"I'm on it." The girl turned away and walked out of the projection just as the professor's lab materialized along with Kendell and Myles's living room.

Sere shook her head. "You've just gotta love that doppelgänger directness. No waiting around to listen in on pointless ramblings."

Kendell set a book on a table. "The jars should be filled with liquid. Simply breaking them might disrupt the mirror signal, but I can't answer for what would happen in hell."

Fat lot of good that does me, Sere thought. *I figured that out for myself.* Saying the caustic response out loud, however, wasn't going to bring the answer any closer. "Is there something we could pour the jars into? Or maybe burn the totems? There has to be some way to break the voodoo spell without risking Bart and his mercenaries."

Kendell turned the page. "The totems are interdimensional—basically, the voodoo version of the World Trade Center's vaults. If you tried to destroy them, you'd only lose access to them in hell's dimension."

Sere wished she had the freedom to turn and walk away like Doodlebug. "Come up with something usable."

In his office, Fisher waved a file folder as if trying to distract Sere from her frustration with Kendell. "I've got the blueprints. I've texted them to Chloe so she can have Bernie study them. Once he has them memorized, they should download into the dragon's computerized brain."

She could already see the blue page with white lines. "Perfect. Too bad we can't do the same with Bart."

"Here we go." Kendell leaned over the leather-bound journal. "Mmm."

Flames erupted from Sere's snout. "You do realize that this human habit of delaying when you have bad news just pisses me off, don't you?"

Kendell put her hand on the page and looked into Sere's eyes from the monitor. "There's only one way to turn those jars into spirit mirrors while retaining the doppelgänger essences in the dragon bodies. Marjory removed the souls of the stoners and sent them to hell while the gate was open, then Madam Laroque instilled those spirits into her totems. It's similar to what your father did to you and Jenna, but in your case, Jenna was instilled into the soulless cormorant body instead of a totem. The spell is basically the same. Those unfortunates in the Laroque basement aren't just high—they're zombies."

The fire that had been wafting up from Sere's nose shot clear across the meadow. "So we can't dump the jars without killing the eight street kids, consigning their ghosts to hell, and pissing off Baron Samedi. Somehow, we need to return the souls to the living. This is impossible!"

Kendell's forced-calm tone was one Sere had heard repeatedly during her emotional teenage years. "While you and Bart are gathering the jars, I'll figure out a solution. Just focus on the job ahead of you."

"Yes, *Mom*," Sere said, knowing the familiar words would have an odd impact coming out of the mouth of a dragon. On cue, Kendell snickered.

Polly rapped on the desk, demanding Sere's attention. "Now, what exactly does Marjory want with your body?

We've been wracking our brains but can't come up with a logical explanation. *You're* immortal, but that's based as much on your soul as on that doppelgänger body. With her inside it, the body will decay like that of any other doppelgänger. And since she's not pretending to be you, what does she gain?"

Sere stretched out her wings. Being in one spot for so long made her back hurt all the way down her tail. "It's never just about one thing with Marjory. Having my body gives her a bargaining chip with the Cormorant and potential access to the professor's computer."

Polly stood next to the professor, who sat in his chair. "But she could have achieved those things by abducting you. Why go to the work of a full-on possession?"

Sanguine's wings fluttered. "Jenna isn't the only one who's been after you, body and soul."

A cold chill ran from the claws of Sere's feet to the fangs that jutted out over her jaw. "I have an arrangement with Baron Samedi. He wouldn't dare try to claim my soul."

Kendell closed the leather journal. "I doubt Marjory cares about your deal with the dead. As the most powerful businesswoman in New Orleans, she's hijacked more than a few ironclad agreements. Exchanging access to your soul with the ruler of the afterlife might gain her serious voodoo points."

Flames curled up from Sere's mouth. "You think she'd offer to exchange one immortal for another—my soul returns to the *deep waters*, so hers gets to remain among the living forever?" Much as she hated to admit it, the plan had a certain evil logic to it.

"We're just trying to see all of the options," Kendell said. "It wouldn't be the first time one soul was bargained for another."

"That was different." Myles sat down on the couch next to Kendell. "We gave Baron Malveaux's soul to Samedi in exchange for an innocent."

Sere was well acquainted with the story of how her father had been added to the *deep waters* in place of her. "I'm hardly an innocent now."

"A deal is a deal," Myles said. "I'll reinforce our position with Baron Samedi. He's not going to be happy that Marjory is planning multiple immortals."

Sere didn't need another contestant in the battle for life. "Go easy on him. If he thinks she's making a move on the afterlife, he might come tearing into life with an army of the dead. I've got enough to contend with as it is."

Myles's expression eased from harsh determination to fatherly compassion. "He'll listen to me. You need to stay focused on stopping Marjory."

10

_D_oodlebug repeatedly turned the throttle of the old Harley as far as it would go in a futile attempt at making the motorcycle go faster. "If people can build a vehicle that can do two hundred miles an hour, why would anyone bother with something that can't even get out of its own way?" An eighteen-wheel logging truck zoomed past her in the opposite direction, nearly knocking the bike off the road in its wake.

Being little more than a messenger girl pissed Doodlebug off. "At least in hell, I had a say in my missions." She zoomed past the small ramshackle bars. Stopping at them on the way down to Joe's cabin had proven excruciatingly boring. More than once, she wanted to scream out that she was the Doppel Avenger, out to rid the world of demons, but the drunks would have just laughed in her face. Being hit on by the fat tubs was even worse. They all wanted to be her "daddy," as if that was somehow supposed to be a turn-on. Not one of them had mentioned running across a devil out in the swamp.

"This is ridiculous." She leaned low over the gas tank and clamped her legs over the throbbing engine. If she was going to find Aloysius, she'd have to take charge of the hunt. Sere's father might have been hell's original devil, but that didn't give her any insight into how the monsters thought. Though a worthy mentor and inspiration, Sere didn't have half of the fighting experience that Doodlebug had. People had always been watching out for Sere in hell then laid out life's red carpet for her escape. "Hell's little princess."

By contrast, Doodlebug saw herself as an exact representation of her real: a street kid who had to use her wits and skills to survive. As she rounded a bend in the road, she spotted the sign for Riley's bar. She had to take charge of her situation, but that didn't mean she had to refuse help. She swung the glorified motor scooter into the dirt parking lot and killed the twin pistons that created more vibration than speed.

Pushing her way through the swinging doors, she felt like a gunfighter ready for action. She sidled up to the end of the bar, hoping not to draw too much attention to herself from the drunks.

The bartender's tank top and cutoff jeans were so tight she could have borrowed them from her daughter. "Sweetie, you look a little young to be in a bar. I'm going to need to see some ID."

Doodlebug reached under her shirt, pulled the Navy SEAL evasion knife from her belt, and set it on the bar.

The woman inspected the handle. "This is Bart's blade."

"I was told you could help me. I hear you know how to plug a demon."

The woman's hard eyes seemed to cut straight through Doodlebug. "Bart didn't send you, did he?"

Doodlebug doubted she would have lied to the woman even if such a deception was in her nature. "Sere did. Bart's working with her. We exchanged weapons as a sign of mutual trust and validation. Now, are you going to help me or not?"

Riley used the hand tap to dispense Coke into an ice-filled glass. "That depends. What do you need?"

Doodlebug wanted to ask her to add rum to the soda, but she thought better of it, not wanting to drink while asking for help. "There's a devil on the loose, and I'm pretty sure he's up here somewhere."

"How do you know?"

"Call it a hunch." The queasiness in Doodlebug's gut had been getting more intense the closer she got to the swamp. Bart might have been right. If Aloysius was stressed, she might be feeling the effects.

Riley picked the knife back up and aimed it at Doodlebug. "You do realize that Bart's navy training doesn't come along with the weapon, right? I know a little bit about hell's hierarchy of doppelgänger to demon to devil. Even Bart wouldn't be so bold as to go up against an immortal with only this knife."

Doodlebug wanted to reach for the weapon. "Don't talk to me like I'm a child. I'm not going to kill the asshole, just see what he's up to. Though if it's killing that lights your fire, once I figure out what Aloysius is doing,

I'm headed back to New Orleans to deal with his brothers and sisters."

"Sounds like your plan requires more than just one bartender."

Doodlebug looked down the counter at the overfed, drunk gator hunters. "I can use all of the help I can get, assuming it *is* help. I don't need a bunch of lard-ass bumbling swamp toads announcing my presence."

"You're a snarky little bitch," the closest tub said, his slurred speech indicating that he'd been on the stool for longer than the half-empty beer in front of him. "You remind me of that other snarky bitch. You two related?"

Riley slowly turned from her customer to Doodlebug. "Cody has a point. You're not from around these parts, are you? I'd guess somewhere closer to where that bitch Sere called home."

With Riley still fondling Bart's knife like it was the big man's dick, Doodlebug kept her hands on the edge of the bar. "It's my understanding that you all owe her a debt of gratitude. I saw a number of new trucks and boat trailers in the parking lot. They wouldn't have anything to do with the crawfish extravaganza she led you to, now, would they?"

Lard Ass's stool sounded like it was bending in half as he turned toward her. "That's between us and her, and you haven't answered the question, little missy."

Doodlebug snatched the knife from Riley and aimed it at the talking flesh pot. "I'm from hell, if that's what you want to know, and I'll happily take on the whole lot of you."

Riley put her hands on the bar. "This doesn't have to turn violent. Tell us about this devil you're hunting."

Doodlebug didn't break eye contact with the overweight gator hunter, nor did she lower her weapon. "He's a city boy but knows his way around the swamp."

The big man took a swig of his beer as if having a knife pointed at him was a common occurrence. "So he'll be hiding out in a building, not roughing it in the weeds. That's a starting point."

The feeling of being sick to her stomach ratcheted up by a factor of ten. The most logical place to start looking was where she'd last seen Aloysius. Since no one had bothered searching the island, there was a possibility he was still there. "There is a cabin deep in the swamp that he would know is empty."

"I know the one." Cody set the empty glass mug on the bar. "What do I get if I boat you out there?"

Riley snatched the glass and tossed it in the sink. "How about a break on your bar tab?"

"Thanks." Doodlebug finally stashed her knife back in her pants. Riley's offer to give one of her obviously valued customers a break on his tab was likely as close to an agreement as she was going to get from the sexy bartender. She just hoped the woman's help extended beyond the cash register.

AFTER HOURS STUCK in the metal-hulled swamp boat, tooling along the rivers under the blazing sun, Doodlebug was the first to hop out and onto the island that had been the scene of so much activity in hell. "Wait for me in the field. If this goes badly, I'll need you to get word to Sere's friends." Though Sere had told her simply to find the devil and not make contact, she wasn't the boss in all things, living and damned, that she thought she was. "I'm gonna go talk to the asshole."

Riley pulled the cell phone out from the hip of her cutoffs. "Bart gave me the emergency number."

Doodlebug eyed the rifle in the boat hull, wondering if Riley would part with it, but if the conversation resulted in battle, the weapon would be better used to cover their escape than in combat. "Keep that thing handy. You won't be able to kill him, but you might slow him down."

"What about you? I hope you're not relying on some supernatural ability imprinted on Bart's knife," Riley said.

"I can take care of myself." She headed off through the tall grass. Though the queasy feeling made Doodlebug certain Aloysius was up in the tree, she didn't sense any hostility from him.

"We'll be waiting," Riley called out.

Doodlebug climbed the boards nailed to the tree trunk. The funky cabin that hung in the branches looked more like pieces of a house than an actual dwelling. "If you're in there, don't shoot me. I just want to talk." She slowly pushed on the trap door leading up to the front porch.

Aloysius looked like a giant as he towered over her. "So you found me."

She climbed out of the hole to face him. "It wasn't all that hard. I couldn't imagine you blindly doing what Marjory told you to like the other little monsters."

He led her back into the peculiarly angled cabin. "Those

flying flameheads were answering Marjory's siren call like dogs to a whistle. They went through the connected vaults. Since I'd already achieved real-doppelgänger union, I chose the swamp hellmouth instead."

"I figured as much." Doodlebug wondered how the others had been so stupid as to not check the island, but then, they had been a little preoccupied at the time. "So you've just been squatting out in the swamp?"

Aloysius had a sulking shadow-hugging countenance that was more like a homeless person than a devil. "The best place to hide is somewhere that's already been searched."

"But why hide at all? You're the devil."

His sneer had all of the menace of a sick rabbit. "What does that even mean? If I get hurt, I can heal the wound. I can also manifest this body into any age I want, but those aren't exactly superpowers."

Doodlebug sat on the couch pressed at a precarious angle against the wall. "Doesn't your great-aunt have big plans for you?"

"Why do you think I'm hiding? I'm a pawn pretending to be a king." He leaned against the wall with his arms folded. "How much do you know about my family?"

"More than I'd like to," Doodlebug said, hoping to cut that line of conversation short. She hadn't enlisted the swamp assholes and spent the day on the water just to listen to a family history.

"Those people that surround Sere are real idiots. Have you noticed that?"

At least he hadn't started off at some point in the distant past. "While I agree with you, why would you say that?"

"They gave my ancestor exactly what he wanted."

Though any form of education that didn't involve staying alive bored her, she couldn't help wondering where he was going with his story. "I assume you mean Baron Malveaux. From what I've been told, they dragged his sorry ass to the *deep waters*."

Aloysius scrunched up his face and shook his head "That was his own damn fault. After having gone through this transformation, I've had some time to consider my ancestor. He was the most powerful man in New Orleans—impressive but hardly a world leader. Then he stole a magic cane and took over Guinee. Again, that's nothing to sneer at, but ruling purgatory doesn't qualify as being a god, and gaining the position through theft doesn't equal being qualified for handling the responsibilities. Even so, he was just a gatekeeper for the halfway house between the living and the dead."

Doodlebug fell back against the cushions. "You're starting to bore me."

He either didn't notice her irritation or didn't care. "Those busybodies gave him what he wanted most. They built a whole damn dimension then dumped his soul into it. He didn't *work* to become hell's devil. The title practically fell in his lap."

She hadn't thought of it that way, but then, she'd never worried too much about what hell had been like before she manifested into it. "I still don't see how that has anything to do with you hiding out in the swamp."

"My great-aunt doesn't want to just copy what our ancestor did—she wants to surpass him."

"Boring." Doodlebug drew out the vowels to express her annoyance.

"Baron Malveaux returned to life from hell with the expectation of ruling over it—achieving the ruling trifecta. To one-up him, Marjory wants to rule all three dimensions simultaneously."

Though the story still didn't explain anything, Doodlebug could see how the pieces fit together. "So that's why she left her doppelgänger in hell?"

"Now we're getting somewhere." He uncrossed his arms and started waving his hands as he talked. "She can't bond with her mirror and leave her in hell at the same time. And she can't become an immortal in that body without her puppet."

Doodlebug bit her lip while thinking, which was not an activity she enjoyed. "You think she wanted *your* body? That's rich. She already stole Sere's."

"You think she wants to spend eternity in the form of that skinny, skanky slut? Our family has spent generations of breeding to achieve the perfect body."

Puke, Doodlebug thought. "A little full of yourself, aren't you?"

He pushed off from the wall and spread his arms as if displaying his magnificence. "Actually, no. *I* didn't have anything to do with this body. That's partially my point. *I* don't matter. My soul-spirit-body combination is complete. When she's ready, Marjory will inject her soul into me as a parasite intent on taking over my host body. I'm not delusional. She's a far more powerful spirit than I am. I'll end up spending eternity in some dark corner of this brain as nothing more than the mechanic holding things together. With her banking connections and no time restrictions, she'll take over a lot more than just New Orleans."

Doodlebug could see where Aloysius was headed. "As an eighty-year-old woman, she'd never command the kind of political power she would as an attractive thirtysomething man."

"So now you see the first two legs of her plan—control of hell and control of life."

Of the three interconnected dimensions, the voodoo realm had never interested Doodlebug in the slightest. It wasn't as if her spirit was ever going to be cast into the hands of the loas of the dead. "That leaves Guinee. I don't see how she could expect to take on those loa holes."

"That's what you need to figure out. I can't be expected to have all of the answers, but if she has taken over Sere's body, that would be a powerful bargaining chip. At the very least, it should be enough to get Baron Samedi's attention."

Doodlebug looked around the dingy dwelling. "And what about you? You must want something, or you would never have agreed to becoming immortal."

"That wasn't my idea. I'm just trying to survive. I suppose I've got too much of my grandfather's ethics in me, or maybe it was my connection to you. Either way, I've got no stomach for what Marjory has in mind. Immortality was like a carnival prize, or maybe I was the stuffed animal. I don't even know anymore, but now that I have it, all I can see are the drawbacks. I don't want to live forever."

"So you're saying you are *not* a devil?" Doodlebug's views were becoming muddled. She'd believed in a clear delineation between a doppelgänger demon and a devil out to take over the world of the living. The former would have acquired self-will but succumbed to hell's influence, and the latter would be determined to spend all eternity achieving dominance. But this conversation with Aloysius made the two categories swirl together in her mind.

He looked around the room. "Clearly, right now I'm not a threat to anyone. Given time—which I have an unlimited amount of—I could acquire the knowledge, money, and power to take control. The ambitious quickly discover that they have a very short lifetime relative to their desires. But let me ask you: what if someone wasn't out to rule the living? Would you still consider that immortal a devil?"

"You're referring to Sere?"

"Or me."

As a doppelgänger, all she knew were the driving forces of surviving hell. "I don't know if focusing on the good would be sustainable. I can only define a devil by his deeds. While you were burning my spirit in the fires of hell to achieve immortality, I considered you a devil. Now I'm not so sure."

He lowered his head and nodded. "I'm sorry for what I put you through."

Apologies weren't something Doodlebug understood. They required empathy, and in hell, it was every doppelgänger for herself. She took hold of the tattered armrest of the couch and pulled her body off it. "You did what you thought you had to do to survive. I was there when Marjory cast your soul into hell. You might be an aggressive asswipe, but I'm not sure I'd have done anything differently. And since you're not a threat, I need to move on to those who are."

"I just want to go back to my life. Can you do that for me?"

Doodlebug had enough trouble guiding her own existence. "I'll let Sere and the others know of your situation. That's the best I can do for you. I'll also keep your location a secret for as long as I can."

He walked with her out to the porch. "I won't ask what you're going to do, but if you run across my grandfather, let him know I turned away from Marjory's evil plan."

"If our paths cross, I'll let him know." With Aloysius standing at the railing, Doodlebug scaled back down the tree to join up with Riley and Cody. "He's promised to stay in the cabin."

Cody turned his overweight body toward her. "And you believe him?"

"He's hiding, not plotting. It would appear that Sere guessed wrong again. Just the same, if he shows up in town, you'd better let me know."

Riley slung her rifle over her shoulder as they headed back to the boat. "What should we tell Sere or Bart?"

Unable to keep a secret, Doodlebug said, "At the moment, they're too busy to worry about that immortal little pissant."

Cody nearly toppled his johnboat getting into the back. His tonnage lifted the bow off the shore. "If you're finished, I'd like to get back to work."

She wondered if that involved gator hunting or drinking, but as he was the provider of her transportation, she didn't want to offend him and end up swimming back to civilization. She followed Riley into the boat. "I appreciate your help."

He fired up the motor and backed it away from shore. "I just hope I'm not paying for that crawfish bounty for too much longer."

Riley swatted him on his bare knee. "Just remember Sere's warning. No hunting out here."

"You don't have to remind me." He threw the throttle to the limit.

DOODLEBUG WALKED with Riley away from the dock while Cody secured his boat. "That takes care of my first chore."

Riley grabbed the upper roll bar of her doorless Jeep and swung her butt onto the driver's seat. "Is that your way of asking for my help?"

"Well, you swing that rifle around like a teenage boy playing with his cock. I'd hate to deprive you of the opportunity to discharge it."

Riley pulled the weapon from around her shoulder and secured it in the rack mounted to the roll bar. "For a recent immigrant from hell, you understand me a lot better than Sere ever did. It's been a decade since I wandered down to New Orleans, but I'll take you down there if we'll be doing some hunting."

Doodlebug climbed into the passenger seat. "I don't know what we'll find, but Marjory has to be concerned that Aloysius didn't show up with the others. She'll either be anxious to create a new immortal for her experiments or desperate to find the one that got away."

Riley pulled the seat belt between her breasts, making them stand out even more prominently. "From what I understand of Marjory Laroque, her bank must be the most secure building in New Orleans. What if she's got all of her little playthings locked inside? There must be a more vulnerable spot to hit her."

Doodlebug admired how fast Riley was able to cut to the heart of the problem. "You're right. We'll never be able to break into the institution. But she'd never put all of her rotten eggs in one basket. I've already been to the Laroque mansion once in hell. It's more of an opulent showcase than a guarded fortress."

Riley fired up the engine. "Two sexy country hicks might stand out in the Garden District, but I doubt they'll consider us a threat. Think up a way in while I drive."

11

*S*ere glided on the hurricane winds that whipped up the river. She wasn't crazy about leaving Bart to handle the incursion. Though he was clearly skilled in all manner of mercenary operations, hell played by its own rules—though even in human form, she wouldn't have been any better equipped to sneak into the Laroque mansion. The truth was that flying, flaming, and fighting were much more her style. *I'll make for one hell of a distraction.*

She swung her wings in a couple of firm flaps to get clear of the circling birds below her. If Sanguine could keep the Cormorant busy, at least one powerful force would be out of her scales. Though having the Cormorant harassing her could be useful in drawing Marjory out of her lair, Sere preferred not to deal with the two women intent on keeping her out of her body. Preventing them from joining forces could be a full-time job for someone with a lot less to lose.

She shook her head, letting the pounding wind howl in

her ears. Worrying about how others were going to handle their ends of the operation only served to occupy brain power that was best used for figuring out her own part in the attack. She needed to get Madam Laroque as far from home as possible, bringing her personal guard force along for the ride.

First Sere needed to get the woman's attention, and she knew exactly how to exploit her weak point. Being second best at creating dragons had to be pissing Madam Laroque off. Seeing a forty-foot dragon when all she'd managed to create were a couple dozen fire-breathing seagulls would mean she'd be anxious to learn the secret of how Smoke managed to be so impressive.

Sere had to find Madam Laroque's scaly flock of miniature flameheads. She circled the cemetery, expecting to find the baby dragons playing among the tombs. All she saw was the carnage of goblins that Bart had left in his wake. She didn't for a minute believe that the old bat would give up after having her latest patch of carrier pigeons singed. *There must be another flock around here somewhere. I hope she hasn't yet learned from her mistakes. I'm already in hell. I don't need to walk into yet another of her traps.*

With Bart getting ready to make a move on the mansion, she chose to avoid the most logical spot for Marjory's horde to be taking flight lessons. "Here, little dragons," she sang. "Come meet your demise."

She considered the possibilities as she made a pass over the bank. A doppelgänger freed from the life of its real usually gravitated back to where the shadow was originally cast. A goblin with far less mental capacity would likely be even more drawn to the siren's call. Sere couldn't imagine that Marjory would hold the new drug addicts in the same basement as her latest batch. *That confirms that I can avoid the mansion. Where else would she hide kidnap victims?* With Marjory wielding all of the money and power of the Laroque dynasty, the options seemed limitless.

As Sere glided along the river, Sanguine's white wings caught her attention. When she focused in on the scene, she realized it wasn't the purity of their color that called out to her. Flames were scorching the tips of her feathers.

The sight of her angel in danger turned everything around Sere into the true flames of hell. She dove so fast toward the battle that the billowing fire from her nostrils covered her head. At the river's wave crests, she pulled out of the dive and shot straight at the battle between the Cormorant's birds and Marjory's dragons. Like the idealistic fool she'd always been, Sanguine flapped her wings between the two forces, trying to mediate the conflict.

Get out of my fucking way! I'll burn the lot of them to ashes with one breath. Though she was successfully able to control her verbal outrage, her nose and mouth formed a flamethrower that she was powerless to direct.

Like a meteor, she shot above the aerial combat. Stretching out with her talons, she plucked the first two creatures she could reach and tossed them to the ground. When the birds screeched their protest, she realized she'd failed to snatch a dragon. She beat her wings to get back into the heat of the battle. Though the handful of dragons had fire on their side, the birds outnumbered them five to one. If Sere was going to side against Madam Laroque's force, she was going to have to be more careful in what she grabbed.

"They're coming in from the convention center." With sword drawn, Sanguine dove between Sere and a flock of black birds. "You need to stop them at the source. I can deal with these baby flamers."

Sere would have been just as happy to destroy both Marjory and the Cormorant's forces, but then, diplomacy had never been her burden. "Watch your wings."

Sanguine spread them to the driving rain. "For once, the hurricane is working in my favor."

Sere headbutted a small dragon so hard it crashed through a brick wall on her way out of the melee. She made a quick scan for the Cormorant, but like Marjory, the head of the military-like force had chosen not to participate in the battle.

She shot down incoming dragons like she was playing hell's video game as she flew toward the long buildings that nestled under the dreaded World Trade Center. Though they tried shooting fire at her, not one of them had a third of her flame-throwing ability. *Madam Laroque must have Mickeyed a whole aviation convention,* she thought as the dragons kept on coming. When they started showing up already on fire, Sere knew the woman had taken her regenerations too far. The professor's equipment needed time to reset after a doppelgänger's demise. To force them back too soon risked also calling forth whatever had originally destroyed them.

Sere settled on Convention Boulevard and walked along

the long glassed-wall building. As she blasted the area, glass burst into molten shards that set the nylon carpet on fire, creating a malodorous smoke that billowed out both sides of the building and hid the roof.

"You've made your point," a voice said.

Sere extinguished her latest burst then turned toward a black limousine with an irate old woman standing at its grill. Sere rose to her full forty feet. "Your attempts at copying me are just pathetic. I expected better."

Madam Laroque leaned on her cane. "You're not fooling me, Sere Mal-Laurette. I know your soul is inside that animated toy."

Though Sere hadn't made any attempt at hiding, she did wonder how the woman had figured out her true identity so fast. "What gave me away?"

"I'm the queen of double meanings. Your comment about being copied could either be about that dragon form or your immortality. Plus, a true dragon lost to its demon urges wouldn't have stopped blowing flames. Now that you have my attention, what do you want? Obviously, I'm interested in learning the secret to creating full-sized dragons." The woman sure knew how to cut through the bullshit.

"You and your real need to stop trying to make immortals." Sere didn't see any point in drawing out what were sure to be failed negotiations. *Just start lying so we can argue our positions long enough for Bart to grab the totems.*

"My living counterpart has one already. Technically, that's all she needs. Aloysius is a sniveling little cunt, but that works in her favor if she chooses to inhabit his body. If

I can convince her to end her quest at that one brother to your achievement, will you give her the secret to developing true goblins for my army?"

Sere wouldn't have trusted the real Marjory, no matter what she'd said. This hell version, however, was built with the same restrictions that came with every other doppelgänger, including the edict to always tell the truth. Sere had to ask herself whether she'd misunderstood what forced her kind to be unable to lie. If the dogma really was directly from Jennifer to the Cormorant, and hence to all who followed the birdbrain, then Madam Laroque could be as slippery as her real.

"First tell me why you sent your dragons against the Cormorant's birds. I need to know what you intend to do with the full-sized combat version."

"There can only be one ruler in hell."

Sere didn't really care who was in charge so long as the women kept their game in their own court. But with Sanguine standing in the middle, trying to moderate the conflict—as always—Sere couldn't just turn her back on the situation. "So you two are just going to have it out in the air like rival drug gangs?"

"Hell is hell. Why do you care what we do? I want the secret potion, and you don't want any more devils among the living. So do we have a deal?"

The woman had a point about hell no longer being any of Sere's business. "If you and your real aren't working together, how can I believe you could deliver on anything that you might offer? As you said, hell is hell, and you're stuck here without a lifeline."

"My other can't bake her cookies if she can't use the oven."

Sere doubted the two women even knew where the kitchens were located in their respective mansions, but the message was as clear as it was surprising. "You'd turn over the voodoo totem mirrors voluntarily?"

The woman's smirk made Sere realize she might have just given away Bart's operation. "She has her realm to deal with, and I have mine. We rely on each other to a point, but when it comes to taking over our worlds, it's every goddess for herself."

She wondered how far the woman took the term *goddess*. For Madam Laroque to be able to regenerate after the real woman took over the body of Aloysius, the original old woman would need to be kept functioning. The mechanisms at play were more than Sere could handle in the reptilian brain, but presumably, Marjory had made arrangements for the immortality of her double. Sere had the itchy feeling in her scales that she was the one being played. She needed to get out of there and check on Bart. She'd given him all the time he should have needed. Either he had the totems, or he was in trouble.

"I don't trust you, but the deal is reasonable. I'll talk to the swamp witch. If she can add something to her potion that would prevent a dragon like me from escaping this realm, we have a deal."

Madam Laroque leaned against the side of the limo. "I'll be waiting, but don't test my patience."

～

SERE TOOK flight before Madam Laroque stepped back into the limo. She needed to find Bart before the woman could alert her guards. If things had gone well, Sere wouldn't have to worry about her end of the bargain, and if he'd failed, she could still hold onto the hope that the woman doppelgänger would hold up her end of the agreement. The worst case would be if Bart were in trouble. The threat of that made her swing her wings so fast the raindrops left an aerial wake behind her.

The speeding black shadow on the road below would have escaped her attention if it hadn't been for the flames that trailed her, lighting up the whole neighborhood. Sere struggled to contain her excitement and fear, extinguishing not only the emotions but also the fire. With a quick banking turn around the Crescent City Connection's support tower, she dove low enough over the river to be out of sight of the speeding limo. She set down on the cruise ship dock just as Bart sped up on the Honda Blackbird motorcycle.

She looked behind him to make sure he wasn't followed. "Where's your crew?"

He pulled a burlap sack off the back of the bike. From the size of it, she wondered if he'd taken someone hostage. "They're running a distraction maneuver. I figured you might want to conduct the handoff away from prying eyes."

"Those are the totems?" Her reptilian heart beat so fast the cold blood warmed in her veins.

"All eight of them. I won't bore you with the details, but she had quite the demon-and-goblin army." He checked behind him while revving the engine. "They're probably not far behind."

She took the bag in her claw. "We need to get you out of here. Marjory Laroque, either in life or hell, isn't the type to take a setback sitting down. I can fly you out to the hellmouth."

He nodded at the bag. "It's best if we split up. You need to get those somewhere our enemies can't find them then find out from Kendell what to do with them. I doubt I can just bring the sack through the hellmouth as checked luggage. I'll yank Sanguine out of the war between the women then ride out to Joe's old cabin in the swamp. From there, she can fly me the rest of the way out to the gate. When I know I've got control of the area without any Laroque or Cormorant interference, I'll head home through the hellmouth. Now that we have Marjory by the totems, she can't raise a new immortal, which means there's no point in you staying in hell either. I'll tell Sanguine to wait for you out on her island. We need to confront your body abductor on her own turf."

She marveled at his command of the problem. "You've been giving this some thought."

"Combat helps me focus. I'm done pussyfooting around with this woman. We've seen what we need to see in hell. The next conflict is going to be back among the living, and we'll need to be at full force. I'm certainly not leaving the retrieval of your body in Doodlebug's hands."

The plan was too well-thought-out for her to argue, though she hated leaving him again. "Just be careful."

He gunned the engine and spun the back tire toward her.

"Weren't you the one who always said *careful* and *hell* were mutually exclusive?" He smoked the tire on the wet concrete before she had time to respond.

Bart swung the bike back toward the Quarter. Though he was speeding straight into a fight between hell's most powerful forces, once he pulled Sanguine from the trenches, Sere would see that he was safely back where he belonged. He was right. Nothing they were doing in hell was helping her get her body back.

She lifted the sack. The rumbling of the wooden heads as they banged against each other sounded like thundering voices from the trapped souls. "Why can't this ever be simple?"

12

*S*ere hated retracing her flight, but as long as she was hauling the totems, there was only one place where she could talk to Kendell without alerting either version of Marjory Laroque.

As she flew over the swamp, the bag grew heavier and heavier. *I'm human in origin, this body is part science and part Wiccan magic, and these friggin' totems are voodoo. The weight must have to do with the conflicting systems.* She cleared the final line of trees before swooping down toward the meadow. Her eyes, ears, and lungs burned. She dropped the bag before her landing knoll, grateful to be back where Chloe could help.

Putting her legs down for the landing, she ended up face-first in the waterlogged ground then did a somersault onto her back. "Fuck me." Everything hurt.

Chloe ran out from the tree line. "Just lie there for a minute. You'll be okay."

"The hell I will." Instead of a raspy reptilian voice, Sere heard the uncomfortable tones of a human man. "What's happening to me?"

The swamp witch leaned down next to her. After having seen the woman as a small human, having her loom over her felt like staring at a giant. "You burned out Smoke's battery. With all of the flying and fighting, you've exhausted the magic that made him a dragon. We're down to Bernie's physical projection, which—due to being equal in size to the real man—is much easier to manifest."

"Please stop talking." Sere's ears felt like a freight train was using them as a tunnel through her brain. She pointed out toward the field. "Voodoo totems."

"Right." Chloe looked up and over Sere. "I'll raise Kendell."

Sere struggled to sit up in the rain. Though she'd only been a dragon for a short time, being back in a human body with all of its sensitivities, aches, and limitations was nearly as bad as being in hell. With Chloe nothing more than a ghost, Sere forced herself to her feet. She had to check on the totems. They ran the risk of leaking ghosts after their race with Bart through the city streets and their rough landing with Sere.

She carefully opened the bag and lifted each rough-hewn voodoo sculpture. With their nail-head hair bent in all directions, the old wooden heads looked like they'd had a difficult flight, but each of the precious blue jars that nestled in the chest cavities was undamaged. "Well, the good news is the totems are safe."

"And I guess we can all see the bad news," Kendell said.

Sere swung around toward were Chloe stood and saw Kendell standing along with a holographic office full of people. "So long as you've got an answer for what to do with these trapped spirits, my physical form shouldn't be an issue." Sere really didn't want to hear about how she'd flubbed up being a dragon, especially not from the people who'd started this whole hellish nightmare.

Myles put his hand on Kendell's back. The gesture of support was one Sere had seen throughout her life. Kendell looked at him and smiled before turning back to Sere. "The only answer I could come up with was to directly undo what Marjory did. If Sanguine reopens the hellmouth, their souls can return to their bodies. First, though, we're going to have to round up the zombies. The totems need to be loaded one by one into your vault while the zombies step into the one in the bank basement."

Is that all? Sere thought but kept the question to herself. Getting snarky at this point would only degrade the conversation into an argument. "Well, I have the totems, and Sanguine should still have control of the vault in this dimension. Bart figured the next big battles would be on your side of the hellmouth. Hopefully, he's on his way. Have you heard anything from Doodlebug?"

Polly hit the desk with her pencil. "She's not exactly what you'd call forthcoming with her plans."

"And this surprises you?" Sere couldn't hold back her frustration. "Get ahold of her and tell her to mount a rescue of the eight zombies in Marjory's basement. She's going to need to figure out how to transport them. I don't think that old VW is going to do it. When Bart shows up, he can work out a way into the bank basement. He's probably already got something in mind."

Polly tossed the pencil aside and leaned on the desk. "And what about you?"

The battle with Marjory Laroque loomed like a category-five hurricane blowing in from the gulf. "Bart won't stop until he's got me back in my body. Once we've got control of the two vaults, we can get me back where I belong, then Smoke can take this body and return to his dragon form."

"I meant, how are you going to get out to the hellmouth?" Polly said.

Sere looked around like an idiot. "I'll figure something out."

"Make it fast. Once we get the zombies out of the basement, we'll have a lot of brain-dead druggies to deal with. We can't wait around for those totems for long without attracting Marjory's goons."

Sere waited until everyone had faded from sight before reloading the eight heavy sculptures back in the burlap bag. "How the fuck am I going to haul all of you souls out to the swamp? I no longer have wings. Bart has the motorcycle. And Sanguine is waiting out in the swamp. The only other being large enough to carry me on the wind would be the Cormorant, and I'll be damned if I'm turning to her for help." She got up and looked around the swamp again. Even if she could hike all the way back into town while carrying the bag, stealing a vehicle wouldn't really be an option. As she slowly turned and looked around the meadow, she realized she didn't even know which direction New Orleans was. "Fuck."

A loud snort preceded the downing of a swath of grass four feet wide.

She dropped the sack and started running much faster than she was used to with the man legs. "Lefty! Please tell me that's you, boy!"

The giant alligator's head lifted over the grass. His tail wag sent green stalks flying into the rain. She stopped ten feet in front of him. Though he appeared happy to see her, she couldn't be certain that his enthusiasm at seeing a *man* run toward him wasn't based on the idea of a free meal. "It's me, boy. Sere." She reached out her hand, hoping he wouldn't bite it off.

Lefty put his chin down to the ground with such force that the earth shook. His big swamp-green eyes looked her over while his tail continued to swing from one side of the meadow to the other. With a long yawn that separated his jaws so far that she could have walked upright between his teeth, he turned to present his side to her.

"I don't know what magic lets you know that it's me, but I'm not asking questions. Wait here. I need to grab my bag."

13

*R*iley's Jeep hit every pothole like it was launch ramp. Doodlebug's head still hurt from banging it on the roll bar as they left the parking lot. Riley hadn't mentioned anything about the safety belt, apparently finding it far more entertaining for Doodlebug to learn of its advantages through firsthand experience. Though time had no meaning in hell, she felt like she'd been rattling around in the doorless tin can for hours.

"How much longer?"

"Maybe another half hour. I've got one last bar stop."

A line of half a dozen trucks and two motorcycles followed the Jeep like fat drunk dudes pursuing the one hot chick. Doodlebug nodded back at the noisy beasts. "Do you really think those guys will be able to help?"

Riley turned the wheel hard to avoid an axle-busting rut. "I'd rather have Bart. That dude can wiggle his tight ass into the worst of situations, fight through it like a black bear, and come out smelling like a rose. There's not a man trailing us that has his skills, but together, they'll at least provide some backup."

Doodlebug feared Riley was better at rounding up help than at devising a game plan. She looked behind the annoyingly bouncy Jeep. "We should have enough seats and truck beds back there for the zombies, but I suppose the more help you can round up, the better."

Riley bent her naked leg, stepped on the clutch, and shifted the grumpy vehicle into a higher gear. "Cool. That just leaves breaking into the home of the most powerful family in New Orleans, rescuing eight prisoners, and delivering them to the bank. Remind me why I agreed to this?"

"Bart will help," Doodlebug said, trying to think of someone else they could rely on. Turning to the idiots in the professor's offices would only alert Marjory to what they were doing. The damn woman really had her fingers in every financial pie. "Wait! I've got an idea!"

Riley started shaking her head before she even turned toward Doodlebug. "You're like an annoying little sister. Yelling at me while I'm driving is a sure way of landing us in a ditch."

Doodlebug had been called far worse. "I need to get to the French Quarter. There's a CPA who Sere always turns to when she's stumped."

Riley turned the wheel so sharply that Doodlebug wondered if she were trying to dump her out of the Jeep. "Seriously? I don't think financial planning is going to help at this point."

Doodlebug put her hand on Riley's extended arm, as much to make a point as to stay in the car. "Trust me. This guy is a wiz at figuring stuff out, and he's been possessed by a demon, so he knows how we think."

Riley pulled into a bar parking lot. At least this one was paved. "I don't see how that's going to help in the least, but I'll have my guys round up who they can here. Then you and I will head down to the big city."

DOODLEBUG PUSHED OPEN the CPA's door on the dingy side street of the Quarter. "I need to see Montgomery Fisher."

The ancient woman behind the desk glared over her reading glasses. "Do you have an appointment?"

Based on the blank calendar on the desk, Doodlebug assumed the woman was intentionally being difficult. "Nope. It's important that I see him."

"Mr. Fisher is very busy. Leave me your name, and I'll try to fit you in next week." The woman turned to the old computer monitor like she was getting back to her soap opera.

"I work with Sere Mal-Laurette."

The woman's glare turned into an icy stare. "Of course you do. Mr. Fisher is very busy. Next week."

"I need to see him now!" Doodlebug yelled. She didn't like raising her voice, but some messages required more than a polite tone.

The door behind the disagreeable secretary sprang open. "Is there a problem?" Montgomery Fisher stood there in a rumpled seersucker suit, looking like he'd just gotten up from a nap. "I know you, don't I? We met at the professor's lab."

"That must have been my *twin sister.*" Doodlebug emphasized the last two words, hoping he would understand what she really meant.

"Come on in."

The old woman behind the desk slammed her fist onto the calendar. "You have appointments. Why do I even bother?"

"Because I couldn't get by without you. Hold my calls."

Doodlebug followed the man into his office with Riley at her heels. "I have a problem. Sere says you can perform magic with numbers."

He sat behind an old wooden desk. "What trouble is she in this time?"

She took a seat while Riley remained at the door like a henchman expecting an unwanted intruder. "I don't know what she's up to. My task is freeing the drug addicts from Marjory Laroque's basement."

"Have you been talking to Polly?"

Doodlebug clenched her fist under the desk where the man wouldn't be able to see. She'd really hoped to avoid talking about the group of busybodies. "Why?"

"I thought she was coordinating the efforts on this side of the divide." The man pulled some rolled-up blueprints from the bottom drawer of his desk. "I already sent this information to hell. Supposedly, Bart made the same move to rescue the totems that hold the stoners' souls."

"Good to know we had the same thought. It would have

been nice if they'd told me." Though the interdimensional meeting with Sere as a dragon had still been going on when Doodlebug left, if there was an important new development, they should have told her. She reached over and unrolled the pages, which ended up covering the desk. "What is all of this crap?"

"The Laroque mansion." He pulled out an extendable metal pointer and aimed it at the drawing like a doctor looking at an x-ray. "This is where Bart was going to make his attack. The Laroques make a big deal of security out front, but they prefer their privacy when it comes to the backyard gardens."

"I'm familiar with the layout."

He looked up from his explanation. "I'm sorry. Of course you are. I forgot you played a gig there in hell. The door down to the cellar is right off the back entrance."

"I remember seeing it. So that's where the zombies are being held. Anything else you can tell me?"

He pulled a small black book from the same drawer. "Marjory relies on her brother's connections with the police force for securing the grounds. After my online financial manipulations last time, she started paying those off-duty cops in cash. You're going to need another way of calling off the dogs."

Doodlebug got up. Time was slipping away. "I'll figure something out."

Fisher leaned back in his leather executive chair. "I can see it's pointless to tell you to talk with the others. You remind me of Sere the first time I met her. Bart's on his way from hell. He'll take over once he gets here. He'll probably need all the help you can provide."

"Bart's coming?" Riley had managed to keep her tits out of the conversation, but her excited reaction to the former Navy SEAL's arrival told Doodlebug more about their past relationship than she really wanted to know.

RILEY HAD BEEN RIGHT about the Jeep. It stood out like a high school kid's jalopy among the BMWs and Mercedes that lined the street in the Garden District. Had it been in hell, Doodlebug would have known what to do. Life, however, was a constant confusion for her. She leaned over the gearshift. "What do we do now?"

Riley sat hunched over the steering wheel like she was stalking an ex-lover. "If this were up north, I'd simply get out and wiggle my ass. That never fails to call out any hidden security guard, but then, gender roles are a lot simpler up there."

Doodlebug stared at the woman in the dark. "So we need a diversion?"

Riley tapped the gun in the rack over their heads. "Darlin', I sling drinks for a living. If there's a problem, I pull out my tits or my shotgun. Either one usually gets the attention of the combatants. Down here, if you're relying on me for answers, we're all in serious trouble." Between the beer, the blaster, and the breasts, Riley was a walking distraction all on her own but, unfortunately, not the type that would call out a covert guard.

The police car that rolled up behind them let out half of a siren blast but didn't flash its lights. Doodlebug hadn't heard or seen the bastard approach.

"Fuck." Riley kept her hands on the steering wheel.

The cop got out of his cruiser, checked his weapon, and approached the Jeep. "License and registration."

"We're not moving, officer. You can't ask for paperwork if we're just sitting in the car." Riley's downcast look and clenched jaw perfectly matched her tone of controlled defiance.

"Can I ask what you two are doing here?" The guy held his thumbs under the gleaming belt buckle like some pervert.

"Is it a crime to sit in a car?" Doodlebug said. Since their secrecy was blown, she didn't see any point in being hospitable.

"Are you Dooly Buell?" The dude moved his hand to his sidearm.

She didn't know how to answer. To say no, though technically the truth, would require some alternate relationship like twin sister, which would be a lie. To say yes, though mostly accurate, would still be a lie. A snarky response seemed the best course of action.

"What's it to you?"

"She hasn't done anything wrong." Riley kept her hands on the wheel, but from her half glance over her shoulder, Doodlebug knew she wanted to reach for the shotgun.

"Are you her mother?" the guy asked.

Riley gripped the wheel so hard her knuckles turned white. "Do I *look* like her mother?"

He took a half step back from the passenger-side door and unlatched his holster. "I'm going to have to ask you both to come with me."

Lights were coming on in mansion windows. People were beginning to peek through the shades. No one's cause would be furthered by the two of them getting into a full-on battle in the street with a cop. Riley put her hand on Doodlebug's arm. "We'll come peacefully."

DOODLEBUG TURNED AWAY from the cop-car window as they sped through the Garden District. "Why, for the love of God, did you let him load us into this cruiser?"

"We didn't have a plan, and sitting out there was only going to call attention to us." Riley gave Doodlebug a long glare that conveyed what she dared not say—that they still had resources and if they'd taken things any further, those rural hotheads might have come swooping in for an ill-considered rescue attempt. The woman had to protect the barflies, and with her and Doodlebug in police custody, all she could do was hope the gator hunters and random drunks had stuck to the backup plan—though leaving them at a bar awaiting orders didn't seem like the best idea to Doodlebug.

She went back to staring out the window. "Unless things are radically different from what I remember, this isn't the way to the police station."

The cop turned into the parking lot of an abandoned building then continued on until the car was undercover and out of sight from the street. "Someone wants to have a talk with you. Just cool your jets." He got out, left the door open, and walked to the garage entrance like he was about to stand guard.

A large man appeared, filling the door opening, and plopped down on the driver's seat. "Just tell me this. What exactly was your plan? I mean, even if you had gotten past the security detail, broken into my sister's home, and managed to get the dead walking, what were you going to do with them?"

Doodlebug wasn't sure if she should be afraid or relieved. "You're Gerald Laroque. Bart said I should find you if things turned ugly."

The former chief of police's face in the rearview mirror didn't look happy to see her. "I'm only useful if no one knows I'm helping you people. Start talking, or I'll have my friend out there haul you into the station just to keep you from causing real trouble."

"Sere told me to watch out for Aloysius and stop his demons."

The big man turned in the seat to face her. "You've seen my grandson?"

She'd made a promise to keep his location a secret. "He's safe for now."

"How did you find us?" Riley asked.

"Though my sister lives in the mansion, it belongs to both of us. That means I have complete control of its security. I'm not stupid, unlike *some* people. Both Sere and Bart told me to keep an eye out for you, so when I spotted you on the neighborhood police cams, I sent someone to fetch you. Now, tell me about my grandson. Where is he?"

"I promised I wouldn't. He did tell me that if I saw you to say he didn't turn evil."

The big man's nod was heavy with emotion. "Then let me tell you what I know, and if our stories mesh, maybe you'll be a little more forthcoming with your information. Bart made it out of hell. The first thing he did was check in with his drinking biker buddies. They saw an overweight alligator hunter taking *Sere* out on his boat. Since we know Sere's soul is in hell, and my sister has control of her body, I have to assume that Aloysius is somewhere out in the swamp, and she's gone after him. How am I doing so far?"

"Fucking Cody!" Riley hit the car door.

Doodlebug was beginning to understand how manipulative humans could be. "To be fair, he didn't impress me as the smartest gator hunter in the swamp."

Riley took a calming breath. "True. And he's gone up against the real Sere enough times and had his pride handed to him that he's not likely to cross her again. Marjory wouldn't have had to work very hard to convince him to do whatever *Sere* said."

Doodlebug honestly didn't care what the fat oaf thought. "At this point, it doesn't matter. We have to accept that Marjory has Aloysius. This is bad. When I talked to Aloysius, he was pretty sure his great-aunt wanted to possess his immortal body."

Riley squeezed her eyes shut. "So while we were barhopping our way down to New Orleans and playing zombie stakeout, Marjory—in the form of Sere—conned her way out to the island and abducted the new immortal."

Gerald started the police cruiser. "There's only one place she'd take him. But we're going to need some magic first." Before putting the car in gear, he pulled out a cell phone, punched the screen, and put it to his ear. "We need to meet. I'm coming to you this time." He gave the horn a light blast then turned to the policeman standing guard and yelled, "Get in."

14

"This is Kendell and Myles's place." Though Doodlebug had never been there personally, Dooly's memories of the hot bath and warm couch after years of sleeping on the street were pretty specific.

"We have a long history." Gerald parked the police car right up front in a tow-away zone as if marking the building as one involved in something nefarious. "One that I suspect all of us would rather forget."

"What do you want me to do, boss?" the cop in the passenger seat asked.

"Drive Miss O'Leary back to her Jeep. I'm sure there are some people wondering what happened to her." Gerald looked at the sexy bartender through the safety glass. "Don't do anything stupid."

Riley shook her head. "Based on my time with these people, you might want to start being a little more specific on that point."

He stepped out of the car and opened the back door for Doodlebug. "Things were a lot simpler when Joe was around."

She got out but didn't respond. At this point in their acquaintance, if Chief Laroque heard that she was the one who pulled the trigger on Joe, he could too easily turn from an ally into an enemy. She followed him down the carriageway of the converted Creole townhouse, past the black motorcycle, and up the back stairs.

Two dogs were barking their fool heads off behind the door. Even from outside, Doodlebug knew one of them wasn't of this world. The other had the spooky, hair-raising howl of a creature who'd seen too much. She reached for the missing katana sword that she'd given up in hell.

Myles opened the door, holding the small black hellhound like it was an annoying but harmless puppy, while Kendell held the larger animal that had participated in more than her fair share of mysteries. "Come in." He checked behind them before closing the door.

Spotting Bart, Doodlebug had a momentary irrational desire to hug the big man. She fought back the confusing emotion. "Looks like you made it."

"It's good to be back." Like every warrior she'd known, he didn't unload the events like some whiny little bitch.

As Myles set his dog down, she really wished she had a weapon to defend herself. "What's with the monsters?" She tried not to make the question come out as an accusation.

Kendell set her overweight dog down next to the black hellion. "These are Cheesecake and her pup Doughnut Hole. I'd guess they might seem a little strange to you. Doughnut

Hole comes from your dimension. Both dogs have been gifted with long life from the loas of the dead for our help in dealing with Baron Malveaux. But I'm sure that's not why you're here."

Chief Laroque remained close to the door. "Events are in motion that I can't control. Thanks to Sere and her hell-based assistant here, my grandson hasn't been destroyed. However, now that he's immortal, my sister has her sights on him. We have a shared problem."

Kendell led the way into the living room and took a seat on the couch. "You're not telling us anything new or what you want us to do about the situation."

Gerald picked up a chess set from the bookcase, dumped the contents on the coffee table, and lined up the opposing pieces. "Here's how I see the problem. Each of these represents a body and their spirit—be it human, doppelgänger, or immortal." He stood the rectangular box on its end. "And this is the vault. It can only handle one transfer of soul to body at a time." He wrapped a rubber band around the two kings and another around the black knight and white queen. He then placed the two sets in the vault. "Marjory's first act will be to leave Sere's body and take over my immortal grandson." He removed the rubber band from the queen and added it to the kings then took them out of the box. "That will leave Sere's body in the vault."

Bart rubbed his jaw while staring at the game pieces. "Sanguine had to open the hellmouth for Lefty to ferry me across. She's standing on her island in hell with the other vault, waiting for Sere to return with the totems. To stop

Marjory from crushing up the dragons—both doppelgänger spirits and human souls—in order to create her immortals, the mirrors have to be taken out of hell and returned to their living bodies."

Myles set all of the pawns representing the dragons and demons to the side. "Since Sere's body will still be inside the vault, she needs to transfer over first. That's going to be a little complicated."

"When isn't it complicated with Sere?" Bart asked.

Doodlebug hated the complexity of the problem. "She can give Smoke his body back easily enough. All she has to do is step into the vault. Since the dragon spirit is in the totem, it should be an easy transfer." She set the other side of the box back-to-back with the one Gerald had set up then put a knight in each one.

"This is where things get messy." Myles set up the game board then took the white knight and put it on the edge. "Sere's soul entered our game from the vault in life, but she escaped Marjory by jumping into the professor's computer. From there, she was hooked to Jennifer so that the Cormorant would drag her across dimensions." With each explanation he moved the piece farther onto the board. "Simply relying on Sere's body—which is actually Jennifer's mirror and not Sere's *original* body—to call her soul from hell won't be enough. Voodoo won't do—we need the science as well to get her off the board."

Bart pulled out his phone and tossed it onto the table. "That's why I left Sere's interdimensional phone with Sanguine. After Jennifer used it out in the swamp to connect to Sere in the computer, I brought it with me to hell. When our girl enters hell's vault, she won't be alone. Jennifer can call her from the professor's equipment to establish their connection across dimensions—basically the reverse of how she ended up in hell in the first place."

"Wait." Doodlebug threw the game's rule book on top. "We could be springing Marjory's trap. Since Sere wouldn't technically be immortal outside of her body, Baron Samedi could finally claim possession of her once she's out of hell. We don't dare try to put her together again without knowing she can set foot out of the vault into life and not into Guinee. We need to know which side the loa of the dead is on before we do anything."

The dog at Myles's feet started whimpering at the mention of the voodoo lords. "I'll get my cane," Myles said while patting the hell mutt's head.

"Don't call Baron Samedi just yet." Gerald sat on the couch and looked over the mess on the coffee table. He took the black queen and hid it under a magazine. "The only reason I'm joining in this game of magic is to save my grandson, and to do that, we need to keep my sister out of him. How do we accomplish that if we don't yet have her body? Since she's the one making the first move, I need an answer before I'll agree to all of these other shenanigans."

Kendell sat with her elbows on her knees and her hands at her mouth. "I might have a solution. We need another voodoo totem."

"Aren't they all in hell, holding the stoners' souls?" Doodlebug asked.

Kendell and Myles stared at each other for an uncomfortably long time. Doodlebug could practically see the conversation take place in their eyes. "She hasn't been seen in decades," Myles finally said. "Not since we deposited Baron Malveaux's soul in the *deep waters*."

Kendell kept her body tightly wound as she looked up at him. "And with good reason. She betrayed not only her voodoo lords but also the Laroque family."

Doodlebug hated it when people left important information out of their story. "Who are you talking about?"

Kendell let out a deep sigh. "I only knew her as Madam de Galpion. She was a voodoo priestess living in the Quarter—a direct descendent of Marie Laveau. We never would have been able to trap Baron Malveaux without her. The baron stole the original eight totems from her shop. Before she went into hiding, she gave me her voodoo journals."

Myles stared out the French doors at the balcony trimmed in an elegant wrought-iron railing. "We could try her old shop."

Kendell scratched the head of her ever-present Lhasa apso. "I walk Cheesecake and Doughnut Hole past it every day. It's nothing more than a tourist trap at this point. When she disappeared, I went through every hidden door and secret curio cabinet I could find. Unless she built an in-between portal, she's not there."

Doodlebug hated history lessons. "Couldn't we just get Baron Samedi to give us another one?"

"Weren't you the one who just said we need to figure out which side he's on?" Kendell said. The big older dog growled, causing her to switch from a head scratch to a firm pat. "We're trying to make sure he stays *out* of our problems, not give him an invitation to steal Sere's soul. Up until now, I've respected the madam's desire for seclusion. She's not the type to be blind to what's going on, though. If I start looking for her, she'll know it."

The couch springs groaned as Gerald leaned back against the cushion. "Once you get the totem, you'll have a means of drawing Marjory's soul out of Aloysius by using the vault. I can live with that, but until you have the magic sculpture, I'm not agreeing to help you break into either our mansion or the bank. That's the only real leverage I've got to protect my grandson."

Bart crossed his arms and stared at the big man. "And what exactly are you offering?"

"As soon as I hear that you have the totem, I'll pull the security detail, though I can't tell you what you'll find in terms of personal security. After your last little adventure at Marjory's expense, she hired her own team. Once we're all in the bank basement, I'll use the baron's journals to conduct the crossings. Marjory isn't the only one who's thumbed through those pages."

Bart didn't let up on his aggressive body language. "And the mansion? I can't believe that old woman rattles around the gigantic home all by herself. Even if you do pull the guards, who else can we expect?"

"The eight prospective immortal family members have been camped out there. She couldn't take their souls the way she did the dragons' reals. With the stoners acting as power transformers in hell, our young relatives have had to stay close to home until they're bonded to their doppelgängers. It's been something of a kegger for the last couple of days. Every twentysomething in the Garden District has been partying at the mansion."

Doodlebug wasn't sure of the wisdom of sharing their plan with the former police chief, but no one knew the layout of the building better than the man who'd grown up there. "Our idea is to sneak in the back way. There's a door to the basement off the mudroom."

The big man smiled like a little kid. "I remember it well. Not many houses in New Orleans have actual basements. The one in the mansion is more of a root cellar than an actual living space. It has a pump connected to the street's storm-runoff system for when it rains. When I was growing up, the below-grade room was something of an oddity to my friends, but that was a simpler time. No one from the current generation would be caught dead in the servants' work areas, and they'd have to pass through the kitchen to get to the cellar. If you're sneaking in late at night, most of the staff should be gone. That area of the house should be empty except for anyone doing a random munchie run. As for the risk of one of the rich kids heading out the back door, well, it is still referred to as the servant's entrance. If they want to head out for a smoke, they're more likely to use the front porch. Don't make too much of a racket, and you should pass unnoticed. Getting the stoners out might be more of a challenge." He stared back at Bart with equal intensity. "You won't have all night. After her last failure, my sister is playing her cards closer to her chest. She'll transfer out of Sere first. That slip of a woman would never command the respect Marjory feels is her due from our family. She needs to show that she's in charge before she calls in the everyone else. In the body of Aloysius, she'll send the family limos to pick up our kin and vans for the druggies. If my heirs are still in the mansion when you get there, that means she hasn't finished the first part of her plan. These things take time."

The muscles of Bart's arms rippled like he was about to do battle. He turned his arm to check his wristwatch. "The moment I saw Sere and Cody heading out to the swamp, I hightailed it down here. It's a long haul out to that island and back. We might still be able to stop Marjory from taking over Aloysius."

Gerald scooped the game pieces back into the box. "Though that would be ideal, it would still only switch the problem from my grandson to your girlfriend. Without somewhere to put Marjory's soul, you don't have a play on the board. You need either her body or a magic totem."

"There's one more thing," Kendell said. "We'll never get the vault out of the bank's basement, but I want the baron's old journals. We need to do what we can to make sure no one tries to reproduce Marjory's experiments."

Gerald stared at her with his penetratingly blue eyes. "Separating the instructions from the magical item makes sense."

Kendell lifted her dog as she got off the couch. "Then we'd better get moving. If anyone can sniff out the voodoo queen, it's my girl. Madam de Galpion never could resist offering her a doggie treat. With Cheesecake on the scent, I'll have the totem by midnight."

Doodlebug didn't want to know how the ancient mutt was going to find a magical woman in hiding.

15

While Myles used his magic stick to call his ghostly friend and Kendell followed her overfed dog like a hunter tracking big game, Doodlebug walked with Bart to his bike. She'd left the Northshore contingent to fend for themselves for too long. "We need to team up with Riley. She's got a posse ready to invade the Laroque mansion. Even if Kendell gets the totem to hold Marjory's soul, there are still the zombies to deal with. If we go busting into the bank basement without control of them, that woman will sic her demon horde on us. If we've got the dragons' reals, we should be able to divide and conquer her monsters."

He stopped dead in his tracks. "I've been meaning to ask you about that. What were you and Riley doing that attracted Gerald Laroque?" His voice reminded her of Dooly's dad when he was annoyed.

"Trying to stop an outbreak of dragon-flying demons.

Sere said once I found the devil, I should put an end to his minions. Since there wasn't much I could do about the demons in the bank, I thought I'd go after the dragons' reals."

"So let me get this straight. You were just going to waltz right into the mansion and free the dragons' drugged-out soulless reals? Then what—kill them?"

She glared at him. Humans just didn't understand how hell worked. As a former resident of that dimension, she knew that some actions made a lot more sense for doppelgängers than they would for humans. "The thought crossed my mind. But no, smart-ass, I wasn't going to kill them. Riley has an army of gator hunters hanging out at a dive bar, waiting for her signal. We've got enough trucks lined up to transport those zombies."

Bart shook his head so hard his dark-black hair fell over his forehead. "So you were just going to drive them around like a tour group? What exactly was your plan?"

Doodlebug had had just about enough of being second-guessed. "Why does everyone keep asking me that? Where I come from, things just happen. I figured once I had the bodies, someone would have figured out how to reunite them with their souls. That part wasn't my end of the operation. What have you people been doing?"

He threw his leg over the seat of the Ducati. "Saving souls in hell. Hop on. I'll ride you out to Riley and her gang. Once we hear that Kendell has the totem to hold Marjory, we'll need to move fast. Hopefully, between Gerald pulling the security off the bank and Fisher working his financial magic, we'll be able to get into the cemetery tunnel."

Doodlebug got on but would have preferred to be at the motorcycle's controls. "Do you know where she was headed?"

"I know every bar from here to the Mississippi border." He cranked over the Ducati then swung the bike through the arched passageway and onto the city street like it was a part of his body.

Doodlebug hung onto the former Navy SEAL and watched the passing people and buildings of the Quarter. As Bart picked up speed, the street scene looked more and more like a moving impressionist painting with colors bleeding into each other. People were walking, talking, laughing, and holding hands. Not a single one of them pulled a knife to slit a throat. She peered down every rapidly passing side street for gangs of harvesters. "I'm never going to get used to not seeing those fiends around every corner."

"Did you say something?" Bart yelled over his shoulder.

She patted him on the side. "It was nothing." Talking out every thought was going to be a hard habit to break.

When he hit the gas to squirt the motorcycle past a van full of gawking tourists, she felt a little more at home. Again, she wished she had the throttle in hand. With a good twist of the grip, she could get the motorcycle ahead of any potential adversary. His slow pace only made them easy prey. As she checked behind the bike, however, she didn't see a single harvester on their tail. The lack of an enemy made her long for battle. Without the fight, she was just a sixteen-year-old girl with no future.

"I fucking hate self-contemplation." She kept the comment quiet enough to be lost on the wind.

Doodlebug hung on tightly as he swung the Ducati Monster into the first Irish Channel bar he came to. Other than the paved parking area and uniform paint job, the dive would have fit in along the highway that connected his establishment with Riley's. He snuck the bike along the side of the building and turned it into a back lot filled with dusty pickup trucks, including Riley's Jeep parked right up front.

Doodlebug swung her leg off the bike. "That was a remarkably good guess."

He pulled off his helmet and pointed it at the sign above the back door. "O'Leary's. That's Riley's last name. This joint belongs to her brother—a mean cuss. You'll probably get along fine." Doodlebug followed Bart through the back door and down the narrow dark hallway. "I just hope they aren't all too drunk to be of any use." He pushed open the swinging door to the dimly lit bar.

"Riley had to keep them down here somehow. It's not like those guys could be kept entertained at the zoo."

Riley was yelling and waving her hands at a tall redheaded drink of water. "I told you to cut them off at three beers each. What were you thinking?"

The dude didn't seem impressed by her antics. "That I could make a little money. I don't open my doors so fat asses can warm the cushions. If you wanted a babysitter, maybe you should have stuck around."

"Apparently, absence hasn't made their hearts grow fonder." Bart nudged Doodlebug on the shoulder. "Have a seat at the end of the bar. If anyone official comes in, sneak out the back. Being underage may be overlooked up north, but down here, it can mean a bartender losing his liquor license. I'm going to get a couple of pots of coffee brewing."

While brother and sister fought over the nuances of running a bar, most of Riley's posse kept their noses in their beer steins. Doodlebug leaned toward the closest sloshed gator hunter. "Any news?"

"Yeah. The beer down here sucks."

She was already inclined to take Riley's side in the fight. "I meant about our mission. Has anyone wandered in from the street with a story of something strange happening or gossip on the Laroques?"

His bloodshot eyes made her believe he was well past the three-drink limit. "Baby sister, you're asking the wrong guy. Nothing down here makes any sense."

She leaned over the bar and dispensed a Coke from the hand nozzle. "I know the feeling."

One of Riley's team slammed his beer glass on the bar. "I don't know why you're getting so high and mighty, Rile. We can take care of ourselves. You've seen me stumble home in worse condition from your bar."

"That's different." The woman turned her anger from her brother to the half-drunk patron. "You only have to drive a mile to get home. Annie would tan your ass like a cheap alligator hide if you didn't make it in one piece. This is the big city."

Bart pushed his way in from the kitchen with two glass pots of coffee. He nodded at Doodlebug then gestured toward the row of white porcelain cups behind the counter. "Start setting them up. If I know anything about Kendell, we won't have more than an hour or two to get these idiots sober. I just hope Riley and Red don't start a fight so bad we need to call the cops."

Doodlebug stuck close to Bart as they followed hurricane Riley out the back door. The call from Kendell hadn't come a moment too soon. The count of busted beer bottles between brother and sister stood at three each, and Doodlebug was pretty sure the tiebreaker would end up attracting the attention of someone outside of the building. The fight did, however, give Bart enough time to make sure the gator hunters downed an amount of coffee equal to the beer they'd consumed. "I just hope they know how to hold their bladders."

Bart snickered and leaned against the side of his Ducati to address the contingent. "Here's the plan. Doodlebug and I will go in first in case there's any lingering security our contact neglected to mention. When I see the red in the stoners' bloodshot eyes, I'll call Riley to come in and take charge. Those of you in trucks will drive up and collect your riders." He nodded toward the back of the pack. "The two of you on motorcycles will be our lookouts. Anything strange happens, bug out and reconvene here then call me."

"What about the bank?" Riley leaned against the front of her Jeep.

"As soon as I give you the signal, Doodlebug and I will head out. From then on, you'll be in charge of the rescue. We've been assured that so long as you don't make too much noise, it should just be a matter of getting the stumbling fools out to the vehicles. Once you get them to the cemetery, we may need to stash the druggies in the crypts until we've got control of the bank basement. From what Fisher found during his financial search, the cameras down there are part of an infrared direct-link security system, which corresponds to Polly's inability to find a carrier signal she can intercept. That's why Doodlebug and I will lead the assault. Being a doppelgänger, she'll hopefully remain undetected by those infrared cameras. I only need to get to the first one to upload Polly's computer virus. From then on, it should just be a matter of dealing with any personal guards Marjory might have with her."

DOODLEBUG WAS GETTING a little tired of feeling like the kid sister on the back of her big brother's motorcycle. She leaned forward as they made the run back into the high-class neighborhood. "Do you think when this is over I could get another one of those badass motorcycles like the one I had in hell?"

"Not a fan of the Harley? Most people love them," he said over his shoulder.

She knew she should be appreciative of the gift, and lord knew the bikers at his bar were loyal to the brand. "I just think something with a little more pep might be more my style. I don't see you driving one of the behemoths."

He hunched low over the gas tank. "Once we've saved

the world from Laroque immortals, we'll talk about it. I haven't even started inventorying what Joe left behind."

Mention of Sere's dead mentor shut Doodlebug up. She settled in behind Bart's muscular back as he maneuvered the bike the short distance from the Irish Channel to the Garden District.

He pulled up right under the police cam that had caught Riley's Jeep, took off his helmet, and smiled at the black half orb. "Okay. Let's hope he's right about those partiers."

Doodlebug was less interested in having her picture taken. Somewhere out there on the city streets, Dooly Buell was probably already getting side-eye from every cop who passed her. "At the party in hell, the performers were directed down the dark side of the mansion. Of course, that was for a grand soirée and not a drunken free-for-all. Too bad we can't use the same excuse to sneak in."

"That's not a bad idea."

She looked at him, wondering if he'd lost his mind. "Even if I could gather the buskers, those people don't want music."

He pulled out his phone. "No, but they do want kegs. If I can catch Riley before those guys pull out, they can grab a few each. That would give the trucks an excuse to pull out back near the kitchen. And as Gerald said, no one in his family would stoop so low as to bother checking on a delivery. Then our people can sneak the stoners out like they've been overindulging. This just might work." Bart began texting Riley.

Doodlebug grabbed his arm before he'd finished relaying the message. "There's a coat rack in the mudroom. If our guys grab some on the way downstairs, the coverings might help camouflage the street kids."

"You know, you're not so bad to have around on these adventures."

While he finished up with his message, Doodlebug struggled with how to take the compliment. She'd never received one that she could remember, and it felt a little like a lie—a form of manipulation.

He stashed the phone back in his pants. "Even with a plan for the guys, we still need to sneak in to make sure the stoners can be taken out the way we hope."

She followed him along the wrought-iron fence covered in night jasmine. This version of New Orleans had no driving rain or sloshing street-river to navigate, so people peeking out through windows were the primary danger. By rounding a hedge, running down a dark driveway, climbing a handful of steps, and opening an unlocked back door, they were inside the Laroque mansion.

"That was remarkably easy," Doodlebug said.

He peeked into the kitchen. "Most people in this neighborhood don't confront suspicious characters. They prefer to call the police. Fortunately, we have someone covering that angle." He backed away from the elegant kitchen door with its cut-glass oval and turned toward the plain-looking three-panel hatch. It took a good hard tug on the small latch to get it unstuck from the casing.

The humidity-laden smells of mold, rotting wood, damp earth, and body odor laced with drugs made Doodlebug grab her nose. "Holy crap, that stinks."

Bart squeezed through the opening and tested the first

stair. "I'd guess with the amount of rain hell receives, most of what you're smelling would be covered in water where you come from." He grabbed the two-by-four railing and gingerly descended below the half wall and into the ground.

Though she'd just as soon have remained out of what looked way too much like a grave, she eased down the closet-like entrance and into the root cellar. Sitting along the sides were the eight drugged-out street kids. IV bottles hung from the rafters with tubes trailing down, ending in the comatose arms. "Well, each one of them is smaller than the average gator, but the hunters will still have to haul them up those stairs."

Bart bent down next to the closest body. "They're chained to the wall. The locks are straightforward enough." He pulled a leather pouch from his jeans pocket and selected a long thin piece of metal.

"You sure pack a lot into those skintight pockets."

From his half smile, she suspected he wanted to give a less-than-appropriate response, but he just said, "You never know what you're gonna need." A metallic click preceded the sound of chains falling to the ground. "Take the needles out of their arms. We've already moved the totems in hell, so whatever Marjory has locked in the bank basement must already be showing signs of change. Once these dudes are free of the drugs and restraints, we'll turn the rescue over to Riley."

16

*R*iley was already parked next to the Ducati when Doodlebug and Bart snuck out of the shadows. "You owe me for those kegs."

Bart threw his leg over the bike's seat. "And I'm sure Red charged you full price."

"Extra, actually. He doubted the empties would be returned, so he dinged me for the hassle of dealing with his distributer."

Bart fired up the bike as Doodlebug hopped on. "Bill my bar." He hit the gas before the woman could reply.

Based on the tightness of Bart's muscles under her grasp, Doodlebug suspected the next adventure might not run as smoothly as the last. "What will we be up against?"

His shrug made the bike tilt. "The ex-cop security detail shouldn't be a problem, and I've got a plan for the camera system in the tunnel. It's what we find in the bank basement that has me on edge. For an old woman used to high-stakes business deals, Marjory's a smart cookie when it comes to physical attacks."

"Tell me about it." Doodlebug's run-ins with both versions of the woman had been dangerous enough. She held on tightly as Bart swung the motorcycle through the city streets.

The run from the Garden District to the cemetery in the Tremé took only slightly longer than going from the bar to the mansion. He parked next to the church that in hell had always acted as witness to Doodlebug's antics in the cemetery. "I'm so used to seeing goblins among the crypts that I feel like I should be pulling out a sword."

He reached in the back of his leather riding boot and pulled out a long knife. "It's not as impressive as chopping off a head with a katana, but it'll do the job of slitting a throat."

She patted the knife tucked under her belt. "I've still got the other one you lent me."

"I'd hand you back your pistol, but I'm afraid you might use it. Take the second knife. Two are always better than one. I've got plenty of others." He reached into the front cowling of the Ducati and pulled out a serrated assassin's blade to replace the one he'd handed her.

The handle felt good. "I'm honored you trust me with it."

He watched the street from beside the masonry wall. "Just don't get any demonic ideas about laying into me the way you did Joe."

She set the two knives under her woven belt next to her

hips. "How many times am I going to have to apologize for doing what I had to do?"

"For the rest of your life." He sprinted out toward a gap in the traffic, and like a runner who'd missed the starting gun, Doodlebug struggled to keep up. When Bart got to the brick-and-stucco wall, he turned to face her, holding his hands together at belt height. "Give me your foot."

With an extended stride, she landed the toe of her shoe against his waist. As she bent her leg, she was instantly catapulted toward the top of the wall. It took hooking all four limbs around the crumbling bricks to prevent her from going over.

She wiggled around to face him, but instead of standing motionless next to the wall, he was running the back toward the street. Once there, he took off back toward her at full blast, and she realized her part in the maneuver. Doodlebug stretched her hand down the side of the wall. With a vertical run followed by a firm grasp and tug of her wrist, he ended up towering over her.

"You go down first." He lifted her off the bricks and had her dangling over the inside wall of the cemetery before she could reply. Then he lay prone on the narrow ledge and lowered her as far his arm would stretch before letting go of her wrist. She hit the ground only seconds before he made a tumbling landing next to her. "The crypt we need is at the back of the cemetery."

"What about the zombies? They aren't going to be able to make those acrobatic moves over the wall, especially not if their partners are overweight gator hunters."

G.A. CHASE

He pulled out his lock-pick kit. "I'm sure you know how to use these. Don't open the gate until Riley shows up. Tell her to get the idiots as far into the grounds as she can manage. Whatever they do, they *cannot* be seen."

"Got it. I'll join you as soon as they get here."

"That should give me enough time to get the caskets out of the tomb."

WITH GATOR HUNTERS and zombies in position, Doodlebug snuck back to Bart. The man was covered in what she hoped was dirt, but from the smell, it was probably someone's long-dead relative. "You know, I think that's really creepy. And that's from someone used to living in hell."

He brushed the dust from his leather pants. "I've been down worse pits."

She gawked at the impossibly small hole in the bottom of the crypt. "You have to be kidding me."

As his way of answering, he squeezed into the marble structure, held his hands against the walls, then lowered his feet into the opening. "Never been down an ancestors' pit before?" He kept shifting downward until only his head stuck out of the ground. "I think I feel Great-Great-Granny licking at my toes."

A shiver went from Doodlebug's feet to her scalp. "You're not going to frighten me with ghost stories. I just happen to be a little claustrophobic, if you must know.

Entering a tight space in hell is an invitation for decapitation."

His head disappeared like a whack-a-mole. "There's more room down here in the tunnel. Whistle to Riley before you come down. She's gonna have her hands full getting those gator hunters to do their jobs. You might not have a problem with the dead, but those burly drunks spook easily."

Fortunately, the woman was only a mausoleum away. Doodlebug gave a quick nightingale call, and Riley was instantly beside her. "What the hell is he thinking? My guys will never fit down there."

"Your boys don't have to," Bart said from underground. "Just lower the stoners down. I think that's about all you can do. Either we'll win and be able to haul the limp bodies ourselves, or we'll lose and it won't matter."

Riley stood upright and shook her head. "Fine by me. I can't get out of this city fast enough." She eyed Doodlebug. "Looks like it's just you and Bart, little girl. Good luck."

Doodlebug stared at the hole, envisioning the tunnel being much larger. "Take my hands and lower me down." She dropped down, Riley hovering above and Bart waiting below like two different dimensions separated by a hole. Illuminated by Bart's flashlight, the newly brick-lined tube dripping with ground water looked way too much like a sewer. "Why must every place you take me smell like death?"

"Kind of an occupational hazard. Hand me your phone."

She pulled it out of her army pants and handed it to him. "Why?"

"Because as a doppelgänger, if you try to use mine, it won't work." He pulled his phone and did some technological magic with the two rectangular blocks of plastic. "Hold the screen up to the first camera you come to and press Play. Do *not* look at the screen. It will broadcast a burst virus that will disable the security system. Since you're also computer based, if you're not careful, it could disable you as well."

She took the phone back, feeling like she'd just been handed a live grenade and told to approach the enemy's line. Holding the screen away from her, she crept along the curved brick wall. Outside the glow of Bart's flashlight, the tube was as cold and dark as a harvester's heart. At a bend, she spotted the dual gun-like cameras pointing down both sides of the tunnel. Had Bart ventured another ten feet, he'd have been picked up by the security system—if he hadn't already earlier in their incursion.

She crouched low and tried to blend her movements in with the stream of water that ran down the center of the shaft. Directly below the two cameras, she popped up, aimed the screen at the one facing in Bart's direction, and tapped Play. The flash of light made her turn away and cover her eyes with her forearm. When the glow faded, she took the phone away and shut it off before stashing it back in her pocket.

"Okay. It either worked, or it didn't," she called out to Bart.

He peered around the tunnel with his flashlight. "Good job. I don't see any signs of life. If they'd spotted us, there would be a flood of goons coming at us."

She stepped out of the trickling stream. "There's something I don't get. With all of the flooding, what's with all of these underground rooms and passageways the Laroques fancy so much?"

Bart crept forward with the flashlight, looking like some cheesy model on an old-time book cover. "I asked Fisher about that once. According to him, Baron Malveaux funded the city's drainage system. As part of the agreement, he was able to connect his hiding places to the pumps. This tunnel, for example, was listed in the historical documents as a connecting tube that went off course instead of in terms of its actual purpose of connecting bank to brothel. That CPA really knows his stuff."

"So it's clear sailing from here to the basement?" she asked, doubting it was going to be that easy.

His snarky half laugh of derision told her all she needed to know. "I'll go first. Lag behind me a dozen paces and keep to the sides of the tunnel. Since Gerald promised to pull his crew, I think it's safe to assume anyone you see is out to get us. If some dark figure emerges from a hole in the wall, don't hesitate to use the knives."

She pulled them both out so they'd be at the ready. "Where do the holes lead?"

"Basements mostly. Just because the city lists this tube as nonfunctional drainage, that doesn't mean contractors don't hook up to it anyway. Since Sere and I broke in last time, the Laroque family has bought up most of the businesses and rebricked the accesses. However, contractors in New Orleans can dig a hole faster than termites moving through rotting timber. Now, keep your eyes open and your mouth shut. Sound carries down this shaft like a megaphone."

Though a big man, Bart bounded from brick to brick like a kid trying to keep his tennis shoes dry. Doodlebug struggled to keep up without splashing in the stream of muck, meanwhile keeping an eye on him and anything that might materialize between them.

A dark figure tumbled so close in front of her that she nearly plowed into him. Her first instinct was to call out to Bart, but then she remembered about the megaphone effect. The brute rolled across the stream to the other side of the tunnel before springing upright and giving chase to Bart. Rather than following him across the water, Doodlebug built up as much running speed as she could manage against the rounded floor, sprinted up the side of the tunnel, then sprang her legs out straight and catapulted onto the intruder's back. With both knives already in her hands, she sliced through the bastard's hard sinewy neck.

The goon reached for his throat. Instead of words, only blood and gurgling erupted from his mouth. As he headed toward the brick-covered ground and a noisy splash, she wrapped her legs around his torso, leaned hard toward the wall, and rolled his massive body over hers. The resulting thud was enough to attract Bart's flashlight a couple dozen paces ahead, but she hoped any potential threat farther down the tunnel would remain oblivious.

Bart heaved the brute off of Doodlebug and plunged his knife into the bastard's carotid artery. "Nice takedown. We need to keep moving. Somebody's sure to miss this mass of flesh eventually."

BY THE TIME they reached the bricked-up wall at the end of the tunnel, with its newly installed iron hatch, Doodlebug's blades were dripping with blood from the half dozen hidden assassins they'd run into. "Now what?"

Bart knelt on the bricks and put his ear to the door. "I don't imagine you know how to crack a safe?"

"Sorry, there wasn't much call for bank robbers in hell."

He pulled out his phone. "Fisher, we've got a problem. There's a security door to the basement. It's new. Think you can find me the combination?" After a moment, he pulled the phone forward, aimed it at the hatch, and took a picture. He put the device back to his ear. "Right."

"Well?" Doodlebug asked in exasperation.

"In spite of what you might think, Fisher doesn't have every piece of information at his fingertips. He's going to contact the safe company that installed it, and if that doesn't pan out, he'll contact Gerald. If Marjory's brother is going to be any use, he'll have to find his own way into the basement. It's going to take a minute."

"We don't *have* a minute." She wondered how many times she'd have to randomly twist the dial to get the damn thing to open.

"You know, for someone who not that long ago didn't even understand the concept of time, you sure are antsy when things don't happen on your schedule."

She turned the knife handle in her hand. "Tell me you wouldn't rather put your manly shoulder to the door and shove it open."

"Of course I would. But all I'd end up with is a busted shoulder. Sometimes you have to wait for others to do their jobs."

17

*S*ere had had about enough of being in forms that weren't her body. Flying around breathing fire as a dragon had been cool, but transitioning into a man had given her the shivers. Fortunately, going through the revolving door of the vault to hand the body back to Smoke had been easier than turning into the dragon. The totem's glass jar smelled of tar and death, but at least she had the phone connected to the professor's equipment. Twiddling her electrons back into the computer, she noticed every microsecond that passed.

"How are you doing, sister?" Jennifer said, rousing Sere from her depression.

"I've been better." She used the phone app to light up the camera in the professor's office and see the woman she knew so well. "Thanks for being there to haul my virtual ass out of hell."

Jennifer ran her hand along the edge of the monitor like

she was caressing Sere's cheek. "Happy to help. I'll confess, I kind of missed being a part of the action."

She'd seen enough of the woman's past to know that opening the door to that conversation might end up with Sere making promises of future adventures—ones that would put the happy homemaker in far too much peril. "I have a confession too. I've been jonesing for one of your chocolate chip cookies."

Jennifer kicked her snakeskin boots up on the desk. "I'll make sure I have a batch ready for you."

The boots reminded Sere that she hadn't seen her slithery companions in far too long. "Nice boots."

The blush that hit the redhead's face extended down to her neck. "I'm not intentionally trying to copy you, but when I saw them at the mall, I had to have them. Henry says he doesn't know what's come over me."

Sere worried about how the conservative corporate lawyer was taking the change in his normally stable wife. "I hope you knowing me isn't causing you any problems."

Her half smile and head tilt spoke volumes. "He always knew I had a wild side. Our sex life is better than it's been in ages."

Sere needed to get the woman off that topic. It had been too long since she'd held Bart in her arms. "Would you mind doing me a favor? Between getting sucker punched in the cemetery, losing my body to Marjory, turning into a dragon, fighting all of hell, and ending up as little more than an electronic ghost, I seem to have misplaced my motorcycle. There are a couple of snakes in the saddlebags who are probably losing their rattles over where I've been."

Jennifer dropped her feet off the desk with the slow deliberation of a girl who'd just been told she was being taken to Disneyland and didn't fully believe it. "I get to ride your Triton?"

Nowhere in Sere's search of the professor's files had she found anything about Jennifer knowing how to ride. "I just need you to find it. My slithery companions can take care of themselves, but I'd feel better knowing there wasn't a pile of snake-bitten thieves around the motorcycle. My pets can be rather protective when I'm not around."

Jennifer's face fell. She looked down and bit her lip. "Should I change my boots?"

"They're reptiles. They don't have the emotional connections we do regarding those of our species." As the words came out, Sere realized she'd included herself in the category of *human*. "Find my ride, and when I get out of this voodoo jail, I'll take you for spin."

The woman gave a smoky look from under her eyelashes that Sere had seen before when spying on Jennifer and Henry's courtship. "And teach me how to drive it? You do owe me for saving your soul."

"One thing at a time. I need to get out of here first."

Polly flipped on the monitor next to Jennifer. "We've got a plan."

"I hope it's a good one," Sere said, glad for the change of topic. Though she enjoyed her conversations with Jennifer, the woman had far too much emotional leverage.

Polly stared at the floor with her shoulders hunched. "I wouldn't call it *good*, but it's something."

"It'll work." Kendell walked up behind Polly like a prison guard forcing an inmate to confess.

Sere hated that the computer registered time to the microsecond. It made the silences last interminably long. "Out with it." She fired up the remaining cameras around the office.

Myles twirled a cane in front of him, sending a shiver down Sere's software. "Our biggest worry was that Marjory was bargaining your soul for hers with Baron Samedi."

The only thing worse than silence was an explanation of something she already knew. "Get on with it." Sere's words echoed from every speaker in the lab.

Myles gripped the cane like he wanted to strangle it. "Baron Samedi is going to be there. According to him, a soul is going to Guinee. Whether it's yours, Marjory's, or Aloysius's doesn't seem to matter to him. He claims the decision is out of his hands. He is, after all, only one loa of the dead. The other six guardians aren't as easily pacified with promises that you'll keep the living and the damned separated."

Sere wished she could take a cleansing breath. "I suppose I can't blame them. It's not like I've done a great job of keeping the demons and devils in their own realm. So does Samedi plan on *doing* anything or just standing on the sidelines until someone dies?"

Myles tapped the cane on the wooden floor. "He owes me, and that's not a debt he'll ignore. But when it comes to dealing with Marjory, I wouldn't count on him intervening."

"Peachy. So I'm on my own."

"Not quite." Kendell leaned back against Myles.

Whatever she was about to say required her husband's support. "I did manage to get a totem from Madam de Galpion. Keeping Aloysius safe from Marjory was our end of the agreement with Gerald. Now that we have a means to do that, he'll pull the security systems from the bank and mansion."

The pause left Sere wondering if she was supposed to respond. "Well, that's good news."

"Yes, but he's going to be more involved than we'd planned," Kendell said.

Sere could practically see the scheme laying itself out in front of her. "Don't tell me. He's going to be in the basement, isn't he? So now I'll have both Baron Samedi *and* Gerald Laroque to keep an eye on. This is going to be like playing Russian roulette. One of those assholes is sure to go off."

Kendell remained against Myles. "Gerald is the only one who knows how to read Baron Malveaux's journals. We have a shot at freeing you from Marjory before she transfers into her nephew. That's why Gerald agreed to help. It will be a whole lot easier dealing with her if she hasn't taken possession of her grandnephew."

"How, exactly, is he going to help?"

"We gave him the totem," Kendell said. "He'll tell Marjory a half truth that Baron Samedi can't take your soul if it's inside an immortal body, and she can't open the vault if you and your body are still separate but inside. She'll either need to reunite you and face off against you or have someplace handy to put your soul."

"My head's beginning to hurt. Please tell me this isn't another of your long-winded plans."

Kendell stared at the screen. "As I was saying, he'll tell Marjory she needs to put *you* in the totem. This isn't actually a lie. Baron Samedi can't take you in that replacement body. Since your real body died long ago, if your soul is outside of the doppelgänger body but not a ghost, it's fair game for Samedi."

"So if I put Marjory in the totem, Samedi can claim it when we leave the vault?"

Myles started twisting the cane again between his fingers. "Unfortunately, no. Unlike yours, her real body is still alive. First we need to put her soul back inside of it, then she must die. Only after that can Samedi claim her soul."

"Since we don't know where it is, how do we know she didn't dispose of it?" Sere asked.

Myles shook his head. "She's only borrowing your body. If hers wasn't somewhere convenient, her soul would be losing energy. Besides, Baron Samedi has a pretty good handle on dead bodies in this realm, and he says she's still alive."

She had trouble imagining so many things happening at once. "You're talking about a paranormal vault using voodoo magic, not a high-capacity computer. How many spells does Gerald think that thing can handle at the same time? Having Marjory leave my body for Aloysius's doppelgänger form—which is already inhabited with both sides of his being—while I return to my body from hell's totem is sure to burn out whatever magic is in that iron box.

Attempting to redirect her soul into a voodoo totem seems crazy. No wonder Baron Samedi plans on just watching from the sidelines. When that vault zaps out, he'll swoop in and collect all three of us. How do you expect me to redirect Marjory's soul?"

"Chloe put one of her mirror spells inside the totem's spirit jar—"

"Wait!" Sere couldn't believe the people she'd trusted for so long could be so reckless. "You can't mix up all three magic worlds like you're making a pot of gumbo. This isn't the paranormal version of the Cajun holy trinity."

Kendell loomed over the computer's camera. "We know what we're doing, Sere. With Marjory in your body, the mirror will reflect Aloysius's soul. You just need to direct her to the image instead of to the real body."

"And how am *I* supposed to know the difference if she can't?"

Kendell stood erect as if expecting to be hit. "I put one of the shotgun pellets inside the jar. As a former resident of hell, you'll sense it, but she won't."

"You guys really are going for the double trifecta with this one. Voodoo, Wicca, and paranormal science all in one totem? Why not just shoot me?"

"We thought about it," Polly said. "But we weren't sure we'd be able to get anyone close enough in time."

Sere knew Bart wouldn't be far from the bank. One way or another, the big man would come roaring to her rescue, whether she wanted him to or not. She had to make sure he wasn't planning something equally foolish to the exchange of souls. "Where is Bart during this whole magical nightmare?"

Polly flicked the pencil rapidly between her fingers. "He and Doodlebug are in the tunnel with the zombies right now. They made it as far as the hole you and he knocked out of the basement wall, but apparently, Marjory had an iron door put in. Together with Fisher, they're working on the combination. If all goes well, he should be in the basement when you need him. Once you're free, Sanguine can put the totems in the vault in hell, all of you in the bank basement will put their bodies in that vault, and the dragons will be no more."

"It's probably for the best that Bart's locked out of the basement during my transfer," Sere said. "If he's standing nearby while all your plans come to fruition, he'll probably do something foolish and get us all sent back to hell."

"Or rescue you from it," Kendell said.

SERE SAT at the old round wooden table, thoroughly confused. She held a hand of cards, but that wasn't what most attracted her attention. Sitting at the game with her were Marjory Laroque, Aloysius Laroque, and Baron Samedi. "What's going on here?"

The voodoo man in the black overcoat, top hat, and painted face held up his cane. "This is a game for your soul. The rules are simple. First, you play your cards."

She looked at the seven cards in her hand—one representing each of their souls and one for each of their bodies with a seventh displaying the image of a totem. When she raised her head to see what her two competitors were doing, she noticed the markings on the green-velvet tablecloth. A curved line that marked Guinee was closest to Baron Samedi, then outside that one another marked Life, and finally—closest to the players—Hell.

Marjory leaned over the table. "Seems straightforward enough. I play my soul, Aloysius's soul, and his body all as one in life. Sere's soul I consign to the totem in Guinee, where you can claim her, and her body I consign to hell, where my double can bargain it to the Cormorant."

"And *your* body?" the baron asked in his deep smoky voice.

Marjory flicked the remaining card over her shoulder. "Once I'm immortal inside Aloysius, I don't give a rat's ass what you do with it."

"Noted." The loa of the dead turned to Aloysius, who was staring at his cards like a schoolboy.

Aloysius tentatively held a card toward Guinee then returned it to his hand. He glanced at his great-aunt then at Sere. "I'm sorry." He set Sere's body and soul in hell. "There can only be one immortal in life." He likewise reunited his great-aunt with her body but hovered the two cards over all three dimensions before finally choosing Guinee. "There can also only be one person in charge of our dynasty." Finally, he set his two cards back in life and tossed the totem card toward the baron. "I don't know anything about voodoo."

"You chose the most logical play." The baron bowed his top hat toward Aloysius.

Like lying, playing cards gave Sere a feeling of deception that ran like a shiver from her bones to her nerve endings. "What's the point in telling you what you already know?" She threw her cards on the table to land wherever they fell.

The loa out for her soul pulled a masonry jar from his coat. "And now we move to the second part of the game."

Sere clenched her fists. "That's one of Chloe Aberrant's mirror jars."

"Not all magical forces are in conflict." He pulled out a flask and filled the jar. "This is a sample of the *deep waters*. It's one I collected many years ago." As he turned the jar, Baron Malveaux's face appeared, floating inside.

"That's not possible." Sere leaned back so far against the chair that her butt came off of the seat. Her body turned cold as if the hand of death had her by the throat.

"Many years ago, Kendell and Myles used my saloon in Guinee—my gate to the *deep waters*—as the access to rid the living once and for all of Baron Archibald Baptiste Malveaux. They thought I didn't notice. I see everything. Their lie that it was your soul they delivered wouldn't hold up with my brothers if Baron Malveaux contaminated our waters." He turned the jar again. "This is all that is left of your father. He carries no memories and has no identity, and no part of him will ever again be used as the basis for another living being. This jug of water will never again find human form."

Sere couldn't stop staring at the face of the man who had created such havoc in her life. "Then why show it to me?"

"I am merely the dealer of this game. You've all played your cards, but you have yet to bet."

"This is absurd." Marjory pushed back from the table, scraping the feet of her chair against the wooden floor. "I've offered you Sere's soul. Is that not enough for you? Your fellow loas of the dead have been after it for over a hundred years. Maybe I should talk to them. Clearly, you've got a thing for Sere. You betrayed your fellow guardians to save her. The proof is right there in that jar. I'm sure the other loas would love to hear your defense. The whole story of how you let her soul slip through your fingers when she was just a child should prove interesting as well. You've got a lot to answer for, buster."

"So, you offer blackmail as your bet?"

"Sure, why not." Her scoff at the all-powerful ruler of death suggested she usually achieved what she wanted through threats.

The face in the jar turned toward Marjory. "Bet placed."

Baron Samedi aimed the skull head of his cane toward Aloysius. "And you?"

Aloysius tapped on the table with his fingers. "I can be your eyes and ears among the living. You need somebody, and clearly Sere has failed you. I don't have the ambition of my ancestor in that jar or even my great-aunt. I know my place. There's no deity in hell out to get me, unlike Sere. Once you send her back, hell won't have a reason for breaking out." His voice gained confidence the longer he spoke. "I really am your best play."

"An agent, then?" the baron asked.

"You need a better one than you have now."

The face of Baron Malveaux nodded. "Another bet accepted."

Like Marjory, Sere wanted to confront Baron Samedi. Ever since she was nine years old Samedi had believed he had jurisdiction over her soul, but it wasn't just because of her strange existence. The loas of the dead stood in the way of all humanity becoming immortals.

What gives you the right? She might just as well ask why she was the one to become immortal. Some questions were without answers.

In actuality, she was closer to Aloysius in how she'd bargained with Samedi. So long as she was the good little immortal, kept the demons in hell, and prevented the creation of another immortal—something that she wasn't successful at, based on those around the table—Baron Samedi would refrain from collecting her soul. Like harvesters in hell, he was only as good as his word so long as snatching her remained an impossibility. Given the opportunity, he'd break the agreement, and there really wasn't anyone to stop him.

If it had been only her, she would have considered giving up. It had been a long fight and one she had completely failed to face alone. Only with the help of those around her had she kept the world from being overrun by all manner of demons. "I'm not going to beg for my soul, and I'm not going to argue with you." She looked beyond her father's dead eyes to the crystal-clear water he inhabited. "I may be an aberration, but I am connected to those around me."

"So, your argument is that there are those who rely on you?" Baron Samedi asked.

She turned to the dark loa. "No, I rely on them. Aloysius may be right. Stopping demons and devils is beyond my abilities. As a long-time resident of hell, I've found that asking for help and trusting those around me hasn't come naturally. From what I've learned, the living created this hell as a means of dealing with the mistakes *you* made. My father's greed and ambition proved more powerful than even death. But in both his case and yours, the problems stemmed from going it alone. That's the lesson I've learned in the time I've spent among the living."

The face in the jar opened its eyes and smiled. "The bet is understood."

"Now what?" Marjory asked. "Do we up the bets? You really should explain the rules before beginning the competition."

The baron carefully poured the water back into the flask. "No one said anything about a competition. I brought you here to divine your motivations and intentions."

Aloysius squirmed in his chair. "But you're the one who claims souls. What are we supposed to do if you don't choose a winner?"

"Life is for the living. We only claim a soul after death. In spite of what people believe, however, the *deep waters* that are the shared source of all humanity do take sides." He stashed the flask and jar back into his coat.

"What is that supposed to mean?" Marjory asked.

Baron Samedi turned his cane between his fingers. "Now that the loas understand your motivations, each of you must choose a champion among the living. I will consult with them regarding what life wants for the three of you."

Sere didn't even have to think about her answer. "Rampart Thibodaux."

"Gerald Laroque." Marjory was nearly as quick as Sere.

Aloysius sat straight in his chair. "I also choose Gerald Laroque. If anyone knows me, it's my grandfather. I'll gladly accept whatever fate he chooses for me."

Marjory's half-opened eyes and smile made it clear she thought the young man was a fool.

18

*S*ere slumped out of the vault and into Bart's arms. "I've got you." His voice was as soft, warm, and welcoming as Jameson whiskey.

"Just tell me I'm *me* again." Though the sound of her own voice should have been enough indication that she'd returned to her body, she'd had too harsh an adventure to trust her senses.

"You're you. There's no way I was letting that loa of the dead off the hook until he made you whole again."

She snuggled into his embrace. "I hope you didn't end up ripping the basement door down with your bare arms."

He held her tighter. "You can thank Fisher for another act of numbers magic."

She rolled her back to him so she could see what had happened to the others. Gerald had his large, muscular arms wrapped around his grandson while the totem sat at their feet. "You're safe now."

She nodded at the pair with the wooden voodoo head. "What happened?"

Bart helped her up. "Baron Samedi met with Gerald and me in that gaming parlor of his. The three of us shared our cards on what we wanted, and Samedi factored in the vote of the loas. Surprisingly, we were all in agreement, with a couple of stipulations."

After having a computer for a brain, restarting the biological equivalent left her with holes in her memory, but she knew she'd entered her existing form voluntarily. She stared with both anger and satisfaction at the totem. "So, Marjory's in that spirit jar?"

"According to Samedi, between the modifications Chloe and Kendell made, Marjory's soul entered it without complaint. She must have believed she was entering Aloysius."

"That would be the most logical explanation." Her words still sounded computer generated.

"Since she did end up where we all intended, this is where the loas had a condition for their assistance. Baron Samedi doesn't want another situation like they had with Baron Malveaux. Some future member of the Laroque clan drinking Marjory's essence could release a whole new level of hell. We have to find Marjory's body and return her spirit to it. They won't take her until she's killed. I'm afraid that one is going to be on us."

"They *asked* us to kill her?" Sere asked, surprised. In her experience, the loas weren't that involved in human affairs. Her hand slipped down to the knife in her boot. Even though the old woman wouldn't have anything physical to offer in a fight, they would never catch her without first dealing with her guards.

"They claimed it was the decision of the *deep waters.*" Bart turned her away from Aloysius and Gerald. "They also demanded that something be done about his immortality. They said only one of you can retain the power to regenerate in this world. They sided with you but claimed the ultimate solution lay with the living."

"Sounds like something the loas would say. And if we do nothing?" Sere asked—not that she wanted to have another immortal hanging around, especially one from the Laroque dynasty. Knowing what Samedi had told Bart and Gerald, she hoped to identify the old man's intentions now that his grandson was free of Marjory.

"I got the impression it wasn't an option, but from Gerald's downcast look, I think he'd be satisfied to have his grandson be just another human. But I really don't want to exchange one Laroque enemy for another if we can avoid it."

The sight and sound of Doodlebug dragging a soulless zombie through the iron doorway reminded Sere that they weren't yet done with the vault. "One problem at a time."

Sere, Bart, and Doodlebug—with the help of Gerald and Aloysius—managed to transfer the eight zombies from under the cemetery to the bank basement. In spite of her training, Sere was breathing hard as the last one was leaned against the vault. "That's the lot of them, but how are we going to match up the right body with the right totem? We need to contact Sanguine."

Bart pointed at the open vault door. "Can't we just yell?"

Doodlebug pulled out her phone. "Next best thing. So long as the hellmouth is open, if I dial Sere's number and put this one in the vault then close the door, we should have a connection, shouldn't we?"

"Hang on," Sere said. "You need that to survive. We can't risk your number being known in hell."

"You really need to hang onto that better." Bart pulled out his phone and handed it to her. "Mine has been modified so we can talk without the professor eavesdropping on our conversation."

Sere punched her name on the screen then added Doodlebug to the conference call. Once the annoying buzzing started, Sere ran the contraption to the metal box, tossed it onto the floor, and closed the hatch. "Hopefully, Sanguine won't think I turned into a cell phone."

"Hello?" Sanguine's voice echoed in the bank basement from the speaker on Doodlebug's phone.

"It's me," Sere yelled. "I made it out. We need to reunite the dragons with their souls, but we're not sure how."

Bart stood next to Doodlebug and poked the phone's screen. "I'm calling Kendell into this meeting."

"Yeah, I'm here," Kendell said.

"It's good to hear your voice." Sanguine's words cut through the chatter.

"Voodoo and Wicca, united again." Kendell's voice held the same barely controlled emotions as Sanguine's.

"We don't have time for playing catch-up." Sere knew the

two hadn't seen each other in two decades, but there had been other forms of communication. "We need each spirit in the totem to line up with its corresponding zombie in the basement. How do we make that happen?"

"Are the zombies mobile?"

Sere couldn't imagine where Kendell was going with her question. "We were able to carry them here, but they haven't shown any signs of awareness."

"Sanguine, pick up a totem and put it in the vault," Kendell said, "then close the door. Sere, leave the door open in the bank basement. If my theory is correct, the body should be called by the soul. If one of them walks into the vault, close it and have Gerald cast the spell from the baron's journal."

Sere was surprised the answer was so simple. "Let's give it a try."

The five of them cleared a path from the vault to the slumped-over zombies. A minute passed without anything happening, then one of them grunted, crumpled the remaining way to the floor, and tried moving forward using only his arms.

"I think we have a winner." Bart motioned toward Aloysius. The two men put their shoulders to the struggling body and lifted him to a standing position. "Before we dump him in the vault, someone might want to check the remaining seven to make sure this one isn't just suffering dragon-potion withdrawal."

Sere sprang to the nearest zombie with her knife in hand. If the soulless wretch was coming out of Marjory's chemically induced influence, she didn't want the monster biting her. "This one is as dormant as when he got dumped down the hole."

"So is this one," Doodlebug announced from the other side of the near-corpse-like mob.

Gerald kicked the feet of the remaining five. "I'm not seeing any of these creatures responding to much of anything."

The one in Bart's grasp groaned louder and tried to stand, his face aimed at the vault. "That's proof enough for me," Bart said. They dragged the body to the vault, dumped it onto the iron floor, then closed the door.

"How will we know when the reunion is complete?" Sere asked.

"I suspect he'll let us know." Gerald turned the yellowed pages in the old journal. "Here it is." He read the incantation out loud.

A rhythmic knocking came from the door. "Somebody let me out of here."

"Seems to have worked." Bart pulled the handle.

When the stoner fell out and onto the floor, Sere wondered if they'd let him out too soon. She bent down next to him. "Are you okay?"

He rubbed his head. "That was the worst trip ever." He stared around the room. "Where am I?"

"I'm putting the next totem in the vault," Sanguine yelled from the other side.

Doodlebug and Aloysius helped the revived kid to his feet and guided him toward the door to the tunnel. "Wait here," Doodlebug said. "Once we have your partners fixed up, we'll get you back where you belong. In the future, don't take drugs from strangers."

WITH THE EIGHT druggies back to their lives on the streets, the caged and chained demons and dragons lost any pretense of humanity. Growling, snarling, and lunging against their bonds, the monsters, with their demonic red eyes, reminded Sere of her time under hell's influence.

"What do we do with them?" Bart walked along the row of cages.

Sere knew what had to be done but couldn't face the inevitable. "I've never had a problem fighting demons, but just shooting them seems heartless." As she spoke, the shotgun holstered at her thigh disappeared as if pilfered by a ghost. She had her knife out of her boot and at Doodlebug's throat before she'd fully made the turn. "What are you doing?"

The doppelgänger girl held the weapon by the barrel. "What you can't. We just cut their ties to hell. Eventually, they'll start transforming into harvesters or whatever version of the ghouls exist here. There's only one option, and we both know what it is." She backed away from Sere's knife while cocking the first chamber. "You may understand our connection to people better than I do, but you haven't truly seen the depths to which our kind can descend. You've got about two seconds to stop me, but if you do, you'd better have a fucking good alternate plan."

Sere stashed her knife back in her boot. The girl was

right. Marjory's goblins and demons had no place in life, and they would become even worse monsters without their power connections to hell. "Do it."

Doodlebug approached the first cage with its winged hissing lizard. With one blast, she turned the creature into reddish-gray dust. With the second blast, she slew the demon chained next to the cage. "I'm going to need more shells." She cocked the third chamber and moved to the next cage.

Sere pulled the bullet belt from around her waist and popped out four cartridges. She was used to doing the work herself but had to admit that watching Doodlebug's cold dispatch relieved her of the budding emotions of regret.

The girl split open the shotgun and dumped the spent cartridges on the ground. She took a quick glance at the others in the room. "We're doing these outcasts from hell a favor. They can't return to where they came from, can't live here, and will become more tortured with each passing minute."

Sere handed over the plastic-and-brass shells. "I know, and in hell I wouldn't have given it a second thought. I guess life is making me soft."

Doodlebug reloaded the weapon and got back to work.

Bart put his hand on Sere's back. "It's like putting down rabid dogs. No one finds it easy, but in the end, everyone knows it has to be done."

19

*S*ere kept her hand on the butt of her shotgun as she stood next to Bart and Doodlebug in front of the totem containing the soul of Marjory Laroque. Opposite them were Gerald and Aloysius. "So now what?" In spite of Gerald's help up to that point, she still wasn't sure how far to trust him. Marjory was the man's sister, and handing over her soul without some supervision seemed naïve.

"We need to find Marjory's body," Gerald said. "I doubt she left it lying on her luxurious bed in the mansion. It'll be somewhere safe, unexpected, and probably under guard."

Bart's hand hovered close to the knife concealed in his belt, which was only a quick move from the gun stashed against his back. "You understand that Baron Samedi wants her dead? When we find her, we'll need to put that evil soul back in her decrepit body then slay her without mercy. Can you do that? If not, tell us now. We don't need your help, only for you to stay out of our way."

Gerald couldn't seem to take his eyes off the voodoo totem. "It's like you said earlier. When you have to put a rabid dog down, you're ultimately doing it a favor. What you left out, however, is that someone who loved the creature should still be present. If there's any humanity left in my sister, I should be there."

Sere had asked a lot of the big man over the course of her fight with Marjory. "She'll hold you responsible."

Gerald sighed as he nodded. "I am responsible. I stabbed her in the back, but it was for her own good. No one ever remembers the *good* Baron Malveaux did for this city, only what he became. I don't want the same fate for my sister." He finally looked up from the hideous sculpture. "So I'll help in any way I can and be there at the end when you kill her."

"And then?" Bart asked.

Gerald glanced at his grandson. "Let's call it a truce until Marjory's been dealt with. Where should we start? I'm guessing just opening the totem and letting the soul seek out the body isn't an option."

Sere stared down at the wooden head. "According to my paranormal crew, her soul was still connected to her body while she was inside me. The body can't be just anywhere. There has to be a magical component to where she's resting." She turned to Gerald. "I'd ask about your family's properties, but that would probably only narrow our options down to half of the city."

He didn't laugh. "I wouldn't even know where to begin. Marjory used the bank to hide all sorts of transactions."

At the mention of transactions, Sere caught a glimpse of the next step on their path, but it wasn't one she wanted to share with members of the Laroque family. "I might have a lead, but I'd rather go alone."

Gerald nodded. Keeping secrets and contacts safe was something he would understand well. "I'll have my hands full cleaning up around here, and I don't mean just the demon dust. The bank needs to keep functioning, and without Marjory, there's going to be an impending power struggle upstairs. To avoid raising suspicion about what we're doing, it would be better if we didn't meet here again."

"Then we can't leave her sitting down here." Sere nudged the totem with her toe. "I doubt any of us are going to trust the other side with our captive, but we can't all travel in a pack like a bunch of idiots."

Doodlebug took a step forward. "I never seem to be needed, so I can stay with the totem."

Aloysius joined her. "I know the feeling. But if we're not going to hang around the basement, where should the two of us hide out?"

Though Doodlebug could handle herself, leaving her with Aloysius unescorted sounded like a really bad idea. They would either end up fighting to the death or fucking. Initially, the only solution Sere could only come up with was to have the pair stay with people she knew, and that might throw off the delicate balance of power.

She nudged Bart, hoping he had a better idea of how much time had passed since they'd started on their mission. "How far do you think Riley's gotten?"

He pulled out his phone. "I would guess she returned to her brother's bar. Neither of the O'Leary siblings ever could let go of a good family squabble. The totem will look right at home on the counter. Hell, those drunks will probably buy it drinks."

THE MORNING LIGHT was just touching the wrought-iron balconies on the third floor as Sere snuggled behind Bart on the tiny seat of his Ducati. She turned her head to his back and pulled her legs under his until she was in contact with the big man from toe to temple. With her arms wrapped around his waist, she fought the urge to play her fingers under the belt of his pants. "I missed this."

He fired up the engine like he was revving his desire. "We're not finished yet, but it is wonderful having you back in your own body." He grabbed her hand and gave it a squeeze. The way his fingers aimed downward let her know he shared her desire to be headed someplace more private.

"You'd better get moving before I end up risking all hell just to have an hour or two alone with you."

He hit the gas, forcing her to hang on tightly to his muscular abdomen. "I hope Fisher's in this early."

"I don't," she whispered softly enough so he wouldn't hear.

The short run from the cemetery to the CPA offices only managed to heighten her desire. Bart shut off the motor and removed his helmet before tapping her hands to let go of his waist. "You're not helping. I'd just as soon not have to face Fisher's geriatric secretary with an erection."

She reluctantly let go. "You'd probably give her a heart attack, but at least she'd be more likely to let me into his office if she got to ogle you."

He swung his leg off the seat. "Yeah, yeah, everyone just sees me as man candy."

Once off the motorcycle, she couldn't resist pulling him back into her arms. "Not in my case—not for a minute."

He kept his arm around her waist as he pushed open the door, revealing Linda at her desk. The secretary pointed at the back office with her pencil. "He's been waiting for you. I don't think he even went home last night."

"Good to see you too." Sere smiled down at the old woman as she and Bart moved as one toward the CPA's office.

Fisher was on his feet as soon as Sere opened the door. He crossed the room and had his arms wrapped around her before she'd made it halfway to the chair. "I'm so glad you're safe."

She couldn't remember the last time she'd seen him face-to-face. "At least we've been able to keep you out of the direct line of fire this time. The information you've gathered has been invaluable."

He finally let her go. "If Bart hadn't been keeping an eye on you, you wouldn't have been able to keep me locked in this office. Maybe it's not appropriate for a sidekick to say to his superheroine, but I see you as one of my daughters— the one who's always getting into mischief."

Bart let out a husky laugh. "She does have a way of keeping us on our toes."

Sere took her usual chair, with Bart at her side, as Fisher settled back in behind the desk. "One day soon, when this is all behind me, I'm going to work hard at being a good little assistant CPA."

Fisher laughed. "Right. What problem have you gotten into this time?"

"We need to find Marjory's body. It would be somewhere secure, comfortable, and probably not too far away. Though she trusts Gerald, I suspect the site she's using would be a location he wouldn't know about. It would also need to be connected to her soul in some fashion."

"So, a recent acquisition and probably not under the Laroque name?" Fisher started doing some magic on his computer.

"I'm afraid that's about all we've got," Sere said, aware that she was handing him yet another impossible task.

He raised one hand while banging away with the other. "No, no. That's more than enough. I've been keeping my eye on a couple of strange financial events. One, in particular, has had me on edge. Now that I know the other end of the line, I might be able to connect the dots."

She didn't have all day for him to play his financial-bloodhound game. "Maybe if you tell me about the end that worries you, I might be able to help."

He stopped typing and stared at the screen like he'd just seen a ghost. "No need. I won't bore you with the roundabout details of how she hid the transaction, but an architect and a construction firm were recently given the job of rebuilding the World Trade Center."

Sere felt the blood drain from her body as if she were being sucked dry by hell's dimension. She clenched Bart's hand. "Just when I think I'm finally making headway, that woman finds a way of pulling the rug out from under me."

Fisher tapped the screen with his pen. "No one's done anything with it yet. It will be years before anyone swings a hammer in there. The same people who provide for Marjory's personal security—the firm *not* associated with Gerald—are also in charge of keeping people out of the building."

By the impossible nature of the task, Sere knew they were on the right track. "Any idea who she's hired?"

"I'm still working on who they are and where she found them. Mostly, I've been looking at paramilitary units," Fisher said. From the look in his eyes, Sere guessed he, too, was thinking that even with Bart's skills available to them, Joe's death left a hole in the team's knowledge and resources.

"There can't be that many around New Orleans," Bart said. "Is she bringing them in from out of state?"

He slowly shook his head. "If she had, I'd have noticed a lot sooner."

Sere got up and stretched out her free hand. When Fisher extended his for a handshake, she lifted it to her lips and kissed it. "I honestly couldn't do this without you."

He took his hand back and smiled. "Where are you crazy kids off to next?"

She blushed, realizing she and Bart hadn't let go of each

other's hands since they'd sat down. "To snoop around in an old friend's secrets."

～

BACK OUTSIDE AGAIN, near the Ducati, Sere paced alongside the crumbling brick wall. "If Marjory is using local mercenaries, those are people Joe would have known. They might even be from his squad."

Bart pulled out the key to the motorcycle. "His closest cache isn't far."

The prospect of heading to the bungalow in the Ninth Ward aroused her lust but not her intellect. "Joe wouldn't have written down their names. You remember how hard it was to reach Gerald the first time?"

Bart leaned against the seat and crossed his arms. "So, where do we start looking?"

She mentally raced through every hidden location her old mentor had divulged. Only one of them had involved someone else. "Do you remember the name of that lady up in Myers—the one whose garage Joe rented?"

Bart bit his lip. "Madeline, wasn't it?"

"Use your military sixth sense. Did she ever seem to be more than she appeared? I never could wrap my head around why Joe would trust someone so obviously civilian."

He nodded slowly. "Unless she *wasn't* a civilian. Every operation needs a central contract to disseminate information, and any good warrior needs someone to keep their secrets. Using her garage to pick up the superbikes might have been as much about you two meeting as having a secret parking space." He stood up and grabbed his helmet. "If we leave now, we can get up there before the morning commute gets into full swing."

As she got on behind Bart, she reconsidered aiming him toward the much closer quiet retreat with its large bare mattress. "The moment we get this nightmare over with, I'm ripping these leathers to shreds with my teeth."

20

Once again, the high-vibration rumbling between Sere's legs as she pressed fully and firmly against Bart's luscious body distracted her from thoughts of Marjory Laroque. With miles to go instead of blocks, she had too much time and not enough restraint. As they zoomed past the freeway interchange, she lifted the bottom of his muscle-stretched T-shirt with one hand and ran the other under the fabric. His rippling abs flexed like the undulations of a snake.

She didn't mean to slip her hand under the belt buckle of his leather pants, but once it was there, she couldn't deny her fingers the joy of playing about the elastic band of his shorts. He didn't make any attempt to stop her. With her middle finger she drew tight circles on his skin, inciting the familiar male reaction only fractions of an inch from her touch.

"You're going to get us into a wreck," he said matter-of-factly without suggesting that she stop.

"You just focus on driving and let me do the rest."

"I'm just trying to make sure you're not toying with me like you did on our race down from the swamp."

She slipped her hand fully under his shorts. His length, girth, and rigidity had her wondering if she'd grabbed the handle of his knife by mistake. Then it started throbbing. "I'm not interested in competing this time." She ground her feet against the foot pegs, edging her hips up the seat and harder against his butt and forcing his crotch onto the hard metal of the gas tank. With the solid vibration from the 150-horsepower sex toy torturing his testicles, she cradled his shaft against her palm. Her fingertips just reached his clenching balls as the head of his erection projected beyond her hand to the sensitive center of her wrist.

"If you keep that up, I'm going to have to take a different route."

Sere had been so fixated on what her hand was up to that she'd barely noticed the pickup truck that was keeping pace with them in the next lane. When she finally made eye contact with the driver, instead of speeding off, the woman dropped one of her hands from the steering wheel and maintained her position only three feet away.

"I swear I can feel her lust for you. How strange is that?" The zipper above her hand seemed to be dropping all on its own.

He squirmed his leg up to keep the pants from flapping open. "It's a human reaction but one I'd really rather not explore while I'm trying not to get us killed."

She wasn't about to let go of her prize. "You mean like how I get even more turned on when you get excited... It's like a feedback loop." The wind that whipped around his body made her breathe more heavily. Though she already commanded more than half of the motorcycle seat, she danced her hips over his, making her miniature version of his rock-hard cock nearly as demanding of attention.

The motorcycle shuddered as his shaft took on the sudden stillness indicating impending release. With her hand still in command of the man, she let go of his abdomen then reached under her leg to his saddlebag. She whipped out a worn T-shirt without unlatching the cover. While the woman in the truck continued to play voyeur, Sere pressed the white cotton under Bart's pants and over the head of his erection. With both hands on his cock she practically climbed his back in desire.

Though Bart maintained control of the motorcycle, he wasn't as successful at keeping his cock pointed straight ahead. With a couple of quick sliding motions over the rough fabric, Sere convinced his quivering balls to discharge their load. Every muscle in the big man's body flexed so hard she feared he'd lose the subtlety needed to keep the motorcycle upright. But as always, his ability to multitask in impossible situations astounded her. With the section of shirt under her palm saturated with his desire, she settled her butt back against the seat—this time leaving him enough room to relax his ass back onto cushioned leather instead of vibrating metal. She gave the woman in the truck a quick show of the soiled cloth before stashing it back into the saddlebag.

"Exit is coming up." He shot in front of their voyeur nearly as quickly as he'd ejaculated, then he swung the motorcycle away from traffic and down to the city streets.

WITH THE MOTORCYCLE parked on the suburban driveway, Bart remained seated while Sere climbed off. "That was quite the ride, big boy." She let her hand linger on his shoulder.

"Next time, I'll let you drive—the motorcycle, that is." Stiff legged, he finally got off of the Ducati. "Do I look presentable?"

She gave him a quick once-over to make sure she'd rezipped his pants and hadn't left any sign of their adventure. "No messier than normal. How do we convince Madeline to divulge her secrets?"

"Carefully. If she thinks we're trying to trick her into betraying her boys, she'll shut down tighter than the baron's vault."

She held his hand, not wanting to be out of physical contact. "I'll let you take the lead."

He stopped well before the door. "No, you need to be the one to talk to her. Joe's connection was with you. Madeline saw the two of you together. If she'll trust anyone, it will be you."

Sere nodded and stepped toward the door. It opened before she had a chance to knock.

"Oh, hello, sweetie. I didn't expect to see you. I'm afraid

Mr. Gerald isn't here, and most of Joseph's stuff was sent to storage."

Sere tried to imagine the woman as some badass mercenary matron devoted to keeping her militia boys safe. She failed. The gray-haired woman with the flour-covered apron and twinkling blue eyes looked like everyone's ideal grandmother. "Actually, I came to talk to you."

The woman's eyes darted from one end of the street to the other so fast that Sere nearly missed it. "I've got some tea brewing and some freshly made biscuits if you're hungry."

"That sounds delightful." Bart headed in first as if Sere wouldn't be able to take the hint that front porches were no place for sharing dark secrets.

She wanted to start pumping the old woman for information the moment the door closed, but with Bart's grip on her hand and at-the-ready body language, she knew better than to press too soon. "You have a beautiful house." With the single comment, Sere exhausted her repertoire of small talk.

"It's home." The old woman started humming as she poured the tea. She set the ornately painted porcelain cups with their matching saucers on the coffee table then switched the TV station before taking a seat. "I never could stand silence."

The daytime soap opera made Sere flinch. "How well did you know Joe?" Though she agreed with Bart about gaining Madeline's trust, Sere didn't see any point in drawing out the reason for their visit.

"He simply rented my garage, but he was always so

helpful if there was a problem." In spite of the woman's words, her penetrating stare confirmed that they'd found the right person. Madeline turned up the volume on the television, pulled the chair cushion from behind her back, and removed an electronic pad. Before handing it over, she put her finger to her mouth.

Bart sampled the tea. "This is wonderful. Do I taste a hint of cinnamon?"

Sere nodded as she accepted the device. The damn thing wasn't going to work. Other than the ones modified by the team, they never worked. All the same, she hit the on button. The old woman certainly wasn't going to accept Sere's word about her electronic-messing aura.

"An old family recipe," the woman said to Bart. "It helps mellow the honey and lemon."

To Sere's surprise, the screen lit up. She put in the earbuds before pressing the box marked Joseph.

The video of Joe Cazenave sitting at the workbench in the woman's garage with the high-performance motorcycles gleaming behind him made Sere's heart skip a beat. "Hi, Sere. If you're watching this, then I'm not around to help you. I won't speculate about why. You will have also guessed that my friend here isn't the kindly grandmother she appears to be. I'm not going to divulge her credentials except to say that you can trust her every bit as much as you do me. I have a lot to tell you, and if you're holding this pad, that means Miss Maddie thinks you're ready to hear what I have to say. The most likely current scenario, however, is that you're in trouble. This information can be viewed later. Keep it as our little secret." The screen went black.

Caring son of a bitch, weren't you? Sere had never really realized how Joe could compartmentalize his emotions. She held the pad up and looked at Madeline, who was refreshing Bart's tea.

Madeline took the device back and typed out, *What do you need?*

Sere quickly wrote, *Joe's mercenary contacts. We think Marjory Laroque might be using them for her personal protection. If they're the ones guarding the World Trade Center, we need them to stand down.*

Madeline looked over the writing, smiled, nodded once, then deleted the texts. "Well, as I was saying, there's not much left in the garage, but Joseph paid up through the end of the year, so if you'd like to have a look, I'd be happy to show you."

Bart shook his head. "There's no need to worry yourself. If you've sent everything to storage, I'm sure what we're looking for went along with it. I'll check with the inventory log."

Madeline pulled a key from the end table and handed it to Bart. "You might want to have a look anyway. After all, you did drive all the way out here. These old eyes miss things." She looked from Bart to Sere then back. "If nothing else, it makes for a private place to talk. Just leave the key on the workbench when you leave."

He inspected the piece of metal as if expecting some secret complex lock. "I suppose we're not in that big of a hurry for a change. It couldn't hurt to take a look."

Madeline got up and extended her hands to Sere. "I do hope you'll stop by again when you have more time." She flashed her old eyes over Bart's body. "And please bring this hunk of man meat with you. With Joseph gone, I no longer get many opportunities to admire the male form."

THE GARAGE WAS SO clean that Sere wondered if anyone other than Joe had ever used it. "I guess Madeline isn't the fix-it-yourself kind of person."

With no one else around, Bart didn't bother conducting his inspection in secret. "I'd be willing to bet that woman has skills you couldn't imagine."

She supposed he was right. If the woman had been involved in Joe's secret missions, she would have to be a lot more than she appeared. "Why do you think she had us check out this garage? I don't see a single bolt that's out of place."

He turned the key in his hand. "Could be a test to see if we're as clever as we think we are. No one joined our SEAL team until we knew they were up to our standards, and that had nothing to do with who vouched for them."

"She thinks we want to join the team?" Though Bart would fit right in, Sere had never been the joining type.

He ran his hand along the workbench then bent down to inspect the underside. "I only said it was an option, but even if it's not an initiation test, they would want to know we're worthy of their assistance. No elite corps wants to haul dead weight on a mission. How did you use to sneak into Joe's caches?"

It had been some time since she'd subverted one of her

mentor's security systems. "When I borrowed the Triton, I had to break into an old freight container. He'd devised a DNA lock. I had to cut my finger and fill the slot of a screw head with the blood. It was a bear to figure out."

"Clever." He had worked his way to a corner of the garage and stood against it like a security camera sweeping the room.

Though Bart was the expert, she couldn't let him figure out the puzzle alone. "Joe liked leaving something innocent slightly out of place. I think he figured it would attract my computerized brain."

"So, what's the first thing that catches your eye?"

The garage had been a mystery from the day Joe revealed the souped-up motorcycles. "The room is too empty. Every one of Joe's caches was filled with weapons, vehicles—really, anything a well-equipped militia would need. This garage has always been conspicuous in its lack of anything out of the ordinary."

Bart slammed the sole of his boot against the concrete floor. "You think there's a hidden room somewhere?"

Sere never could read her mentor's mind. "That doesn't feel right. He had plenty of places to stash what he needed. What other use would he have for a big space?"

"It might be useful for meetings. Planning strategy often requires everyone to be in the same place."

Sere couldn't make the idea work. "Not in a suburban neighborhood. Joe was very careful to keep suspicion away from Madeline."

"So he doesn't need it often, has it watched over by one of his most trusted allies, and does all he can to make it as ordinary as possible. Sounds like a safe house to me, but he only rented the garage. Madeline sent us out here for a reason."

"We did meet Gerald out here. Maybe neutral ground for negotiations?"

Bart's hunched stance and tensed muscles reminded Sere of a coon dog that had picked up a scent. "Secret meetings that were likely recorded, but it would have to be with equipment that couldn't be detected."

"You're the expert on such things."

"Yes, I am." He studied the walls with such intensity that his eyes seemed to be penetrating them as he ran his hand over the painted cinderblocks. "How did the professor explain how he captured people's activities for broadcasting to hell?"

The mere mention of the paranormal system gave Sere a headache. "Something about how walls and objects record the energy vibrations around them in their atoms. He found some way of amplifying the effect by spiking people's drinks so their energy broadcast was more intense. In hell, those same buildings were used as projectors instead of cameras. Please don't ask me to explain any better than that."

He seemed completely fixated on the painted wall. "And Joe had a direct line down to the professor's equipment."

"Of course."

He turned away from the wall. "We're not looking for something hidden. It's right here in front of us. Come here and run your hand over this wall."

She wondered if giving him a hand job on the road had

short-circuited his brain, but she walked to him anyway and slapped her palm to the white wall. As if she'd put her finger in a light socket, she fell to her knees from the sudden rush of information.

"ARE YOU OKAY?" Bart kept his arm around Sere as if she'd busted her leg. The action was so close to how Henry had cared for Jennifer so many years ago that Sere was able to disengage her mind from the rush of holographic images.

The outside air from the open side door also helped. "You could have warned me about the paint."

"That was complete speculation on my part. Can you explain what you saw?"

She let her hand hover above her head. "It was like a huge file of information downloaded into my brain."

"So now you have the answers to every question you've ever had?"

She gave him her half squint and frown of annoyance. "This is a garage, not a library. I saw every meeting Joe conducted in the room. He also sat at the workbench, talking to himself while he worked. Except that he was actually talking to me. I've got enough information on the militia dudes to get us into the World Trade Center. Right now, that's all we need. I'll sift through the recordings later."

"Back to the mission, then." He stood and helped her up.

It would take weeks for her to watch every one-sided conversation Joe had recorded, but one thing hit her right between the ribs; the paint hadn't just recorded sounds and images. Joe's love for her—the daughter he'd never had—had hit her like a sword between the ribs. She ran her hand over the computer pad on the workbench but didn't pick it up. "Time to go."

"You're not bringing it with you?"

"There's no need. He only recorded the one message on the computer. Everything else, he told me in the garage." She followed Bart back out to the motorcycle.

As he got the Ducati moving back toward the city, she stopped trying to control the tears that formed every time she thought of Joe.

21

S ere breathed in the evening air off the Mississippi River. Not far away, the humming conversations of tourists and the glow of neon announced another busy night in the French Quarter. Behind the newly erected construction barrier, however, no one bothered her crew. As in the bank basement, she had an urge to kick the totem at her feet right in its sewn-leather face.

"So, what now?" Aloysius looked from Gerald to Sere like a kid who wasn't sure which parent was in charge. "Do we just knock on the door?"

"It wouldn't be that simple." Sere struggled to make sense of the number of random people who'd need access to the building for construction purposes and the need for security to keep everyone away from Marjory's body.

Bart picked up the totem and headed for the entrance. "One thing's for certain—no one's going to roll out the red carpet for us."

Sere hurried after him. The lobby of the abandoned building was as dark as the inside of a graveyard tomb. "Breaking in would only annoy those inside. Even if Madeline has called them off, they're not going to respond well to an overt incursion."

He kept hold of the totem while inspecting every seam, weld, and security lock of the door. "With contractors, inspectors, and architects, the team wouldn't bother with anything overly complicated. The palm reader probably is exactly what it appears to be."

Sere heard all she needed to. Her palm had been itchy since touching the garage's painted wall. Nudging Bart out of the way, she pressed her hand to the square of black glass.

"Welcome back, *Mr. Cazenave*." The greeting from the overhead speaker next to the half-dome camera preceded the loud unlatching of the lock.

"What was that about?" Bart asked as he pushed open the double glass doors.

Sere showed him her palm as if he'd be able to see the changed fingerprints. "I had a hunch. Originally, this body was computer generated. As you said, Joe's equipment was connected to the computer that spawned me. Joe flash downloaded a ton of information through my hand, almost all of it based on him. If he used palm readers for places like this, they wouldn't be puzzle locks I could figure out. I'd need the direct access."

"And you figured all that out in the time I was inspecting the door?"

She wished she were that smart. "No. Like I said, it was a hunch."

He smiled and nodded. "You're becoming more human all the time."

Aloysius stood in the middle of the marble floor, gazing around at the grand lobby. "There's no one here."

"Oh, they're here, my boy." Gerald walked around from behind the reception desk. "But they're being awfully secretive about it."

Doodlebug hung back near the main door, reminding Sere that this wasn't her first adventure in the strange building. "Any thoughts you'd like to share with the class?"

"That we should turn and walk away, but that feeling isn't based on this dimension. If I were one of the guards, I'd probably hang out in the stairwell. That area and this foyer are the only parts of this building that remain in a single dimension. When I was in hell, I could walk through a door and step into one of this building's in-between worlds. I'm not sure what would happen in life, but make sure you keep the door open just in case."

Sere hadn't come this far to end up trapped in some make-believe world. "Right. No one goes into a room alone. What do you remember about the stairwell?"

"Fires and wraiths."

Sere didn't know what to expect as she put her hand on the metal door. At least it was cool to the touch. Bart touched the small of her back as she pressed down on the lever.

"Bart and I will go in. Doodlebug guards the door, Aloysius keeps an eye out for anything strange, and Gerald holds onto his sister. Agreed?"

When everyone had nodded, Bart handed over the wooden totem. "What are you expecting?"

"My hope is we find Joe's lost army." She put her shoulder to the door and forced it open.

She'd gotten only one foot past the threshold when a man in a black camouflage outfit yanked her into the shadows. "Show me your hand."

He pulled at her wrist so hard she wondered why he'd even bothered asking. After vigorously rubbing at her palm and fingertips, he pressed it to a computer pad. The readout at the bottom displayed Joseph Cazenave.

"Okay. How can we help?" the man asked.

If he wasn't going to ask for an explanation, she wasn't going to offer one. "We need to find Marjory Laroque's body."

"We don't exactly know where she is. This building is like a magician's box—it's full of surprises. According to the camera footage, she was dragged onto the seventeenth floor, but when we investigated, she was nowhere to be found. We've checked the building from restaurant penthouse to flooded basement."

That came as no surprise to Sere, who'd figured Marjory hadn't chosen the building simply because of its seclusion. "How well do you understand what's happening here?"

"Before this mess blew up in everyone's faces, I provided security for Luther Noire. He ran the paranormal division in charge of protecting the magical objects."

"So you understand about the vaults?" Things were going to go a lot smoother if she didn't have to explain every last detail of the interdimensional building.

"I know enough. The different floors aren't accessible to people of this dimension. According to the cameras, *you* were the one who delivered her body. But based on your hand scan, I'd guess you're not that person anymore."

"Marjory had more tricks up her sleeve than a French Quarter hustler."

The woman had managed to get around the World Trade Center's interdimensional security system by using Sere's body, but that didn't explain how she'd originally entered the building. Sere decided to hold those questions for later. "If she used my body to access that floor, I should be able to do the same."

"One other thing. Your weapons will be useless—even the simple knives. You'll need one that crosses dimensions."

"I know of something," said Doodlebug, who stood in the doorway.

Sere hoped they wouldn't need a weapon to find Marjory's body and return her soul to her earthly coil. Even with the proper weapon, killing the old woman wouldn't be a walk in the park. "What do you need?" she asked.

Doodlebug bit her lip, a clear indication she was trying to process what little information she had. "You, me, and Aloysius are the only ones who could open a door to another dimension. Though once it's open, either Gerald or Bart should be able to enter with one of us. If we reunite the old hag with her body in an in-between dimension then leave and close the door, she might not be able to escape."

Sere could see the advantage of that plan. Not killing someone always beat the alternative, especially if that meant the adversary couldn't escape. "Baron Samedi was pretty insistent that he needed a soul by the end of the day. I don't think he's going to accept another man-made dimensional prison. Hell didn't prove to be as secure as advertised."

"So, we can't kill her in that dimension either?" Doodlebug asked. "Then what's the point of getting a weapon?"

The man clothed in black moved in the shadows. "I don't know what's on those floors. If I were in charge of securing those magical spaces, I'd have more than just mystical locks."

"Right." Sere turned to Bart, who looked to be taking in every word and movement. "The lobby is the only area where there's enough room and dimensional stability to perform the reunification. Even though it's just a matter of forcing the liquid down the zombie's throat, it'd be best if she didn't try to escape onto another floor. Who knows where she'd end up."

"Give me one minute to tell Gerald and Aloysius." He stopped in his tracks. "Do we trust them alone with her soul?"

"No, but they'll only have her essence, and neither one of them wants to see her possess another human, especially if that human is Aloysius. So long as she's locked in that glass jar, she can't influence anyone to do her dirty work." Sere thought about asking him to remain with the Laroques, but he'd never agree to letting her strike out with only Doodlebug. "First things first. We need that weapon before we hunt for the body."

~

AFTER HAULING ass up twenty-one floors of the old building, Sere turned to Doodlebug. The girl hadn't even broken a sweat. "Looks like you've mastered the doppelgänger skill of not succumbing to life's hardships."

"A skill you've apparently lost."

She had to admit that the burning lungs, sweaty forehead, and cramping legs weren't very seemly for someone who was part demon. But at least she fared better than Bart. Though the man kept himself in great shape, she couldn't guess how long it had been since he'd been on a true military exercise.

She stood fully upright, focused bringing her breathing back to its normal rhythm, and shut down the stupid sweat glands. "What are we in for behind that door?"

"You'll want to take a deep breath." Doodlebug pulled a knife from her belt before opening the door. She stuck it in the frame to keep the door from slamming shut—not wanting to trap them in the foreign dimension—and dove into the room as if jumping into a pool.

As Sere rushed after her, she understood what the girl had meant. Instantly underwater, she twisted upward and kicked her feet against the blue-green depths. Light twinkled on the wave crests above. When she broke the surface, she heard Doodlebug splashing toward shore. The girl seemed to be on a mission.

Sere put her head down and swung her arms and feet with as much swimming skill as she could muster, derived from Jennifer's history. When she finally made it to shore, she heard Doodlebug screaming. "You broke it?"

"I'm sorry, my lady, but 'twas an epic battle. Can it be mended?"

Doodlebug held her fists at her sides. "Do I look like a blacksmith to you? Jesus, Arthur, I needed that sword."

Sere finally got out of the water. "This isn't—"

"I'll explain later." Doodlebug turned away from the crestfallen warrior king. "This is what's left of the katana you gave me. Idiot king, here, thought he could use it against a broadsword."

Sere picked up the three pieces of metal from the ground. "That's unfortunate."

"It's the only interdimensional weapon I knew of. How's Bart at metalwork?"

Sere couldn't imagine gathering the pieces, leaving the building, and having the damn thing fixed. There were just too many people involved and too little time. "He's surprised me in the past, but even he needs tools."

"Yeah, well, I might know of a forge close by. It won't be easy, and I'm kind of not welcome in that world." She headed back for the lake.

Arthur rushed forward. "My lady, I hate to ask, but does this mean I am no longer king?"

Doodlebug grew so red that Sere was surprised her anger didn't boil the water at her feet. "Don't be an idiot. People don't become leaders based on what weapons they hold, or at least they shouldn't. My friend and I are going to need to figure out a way to fix this blade. When I'm finished with what I have to do, I'll bring Excalibur back to you. I'm not going to have much time. Keep a watch on the water, and when you see me holding the sword above the surface, move your ass. I'm not hanging around all day waiting for you."

Sere rushed into the water behind Doodlebug. With the pieces of sword in hand, the girl dove toward the partially open magical door at the lake's bottom.

OUT IN THE HALLWAY, Sere handed the pieces of sword to Bart. "I know it's asking a lot, but you wouldn't know anything about metal forging, would you?"

He fit the pieces together as if simply holding them in place would mend the blade. "I played around with metalwork before joining the navy. Forge welding isn't as tough as making something from the raw materials. I'd need a forge, anvil, and hammer. I can't say how long it would take."

Doodlebug led the way downstairs. "Time bends around these floors. We can't take weeks to get something done, but a few hours should be okay. The biggest problem with staying too long is you become accustomed to the dimension. After a while, it gets hard to remember where and when you belong."

Sere wondered if the same had been true about leaving hell. "Where is this forge you mentioned?"

"Less where than when—seventeenth century Salem, Massachusetts."

Sere slowed her pace. "The witch trials?"

"Exactly," Doodlebug said from half a floor below. "And

since some of the townsfolk noticed me on my last visit, I'd be a prime candidate for the bonfire."

Bart clinked the chunks of metal together as he followed the girl. "How is it that you ended up in these strange dimensions? I thought it was pretty well understood that everything in hell was happening up in the rotating restaurant on top of the building."

Doodlebug stopped and swung around on the landing. "Look, buster, you weren't there. This whole area was one big fire tornado filled with wraiths who were doing all they could to kill me. If it hadn't been for Smoke and his magic cape, I'd have been fried coming out of the nineteenth floor, assuming I could have figured a way out."

Bart help up his hands with the pieces of sword. "I didn't mean to offend you. I was just trying to figure out how you know so much about this building."

She continued her walk downstairs. "Trial and error mostly. Oh, and there's this really annoying ghost caretaker. If you see a swirling cloud of dust, just keep walking. He was completely useless." At the landing to the nineteenth floor, she looked over the door. "This is it. I'll be standing here holding it open when you've finished."

Sere pushed through the door and found herself standing on a dirt alley between two large wooden buildings. "At least the door didn't dump us into the center of town."

Bart was snickering behind her. "Interesting outfit."

She looked down at the black dress that covered her feet. "At least it's less conspicuous than my riding leathers." Reaching under the petticoat, she discovered that her boots

—and her trusty army knife—had also been replaced by period clothing. "I guess that's what the man in black downstairs meant by us not being able to bring our weapons. Now all we have to do is find the forge, make sure no one is watching, and remake Excalibur. How do we get ourselves into these situations?"

Bart, in his colonial white ruffled shirt, black waistcoat, and tight gray britches, looked as hot as ever. "We may be in luck, or what passes for luck in a paranormal-magic setting. Watch the end of the street. I see people carrying sticks."

Her blood ran cold. "They're going to burn a witch?"

"That's my guess." He grabbed her hand before she could take off after the village bastards. "Whatever is about to happen has already happened in our time line. The best thing we can do is use the distraction to conduct our mission. This will probably be the best shot we've got."

She pulled out of his grasp but didn't rush after the zealots. "Sounds like something Sanguine would say. All right, blacksmith, where would you put your forge?"

He nodded toward the far end of the alley. "At the edge of town. The village elders wouldn't want to risk burning anything by accident."

She turned away from the low rumble of voices punctuated with loud words of hate. "How did you people ever survive this time?" She wasn't really looking for an answer. A thought struck her like it had been downloaded from a computer. *What if evil could be consolidated into a single individual like my father, the devil? Maybe constructing hell and keeping him out of the* deep waters *has resulted in a more understanding version of humanity.*

"You coming or not?" Bart asked from down the street.

She shook that contemplation out of her brain's center stage. There was work to do. "Lead on."

With her watching his back, Bart rushed to the end of the alley. "That's got to be it there." He pointed at a stream of black smoke that floated lazily up from the edge of town.

"I don't see anyone, but that doesn't mean some mother hasn't decided it's better to keep her kids at home. She could be peeking through the drapes."

He held the pieces of the sword to his chest. "The quicker we get this done, the better I'll feel. Witch trials and their subsequent burnings at the stake don't seem like the kind of thing that would take all day." He made a quick scan of the road then darted across the relatively wide cobblestone street to the next alleyway.

Sere felt like she was back in hell chasing Doodlebug. She kept her eyes out for any pedestrian not at the big event while doing her best to keep up with Bart. After a couple of zigzags along the back streets, he finally came to a stop at the corner of the village livery.

She almost slid into him standing stone-still in the shadows. "Now what?"

He pointed to a round trough of bricks covered with a smoke-stained wooden roof. "That's it there. The coals are still bright red. Our friendly blacksmith must not expect the break to last more than his lunch hour. We'd better keep moving." He darted out again.

She sped up her running pace to keep up, though she wasn't sure what good she'd be once he got to work. "What do you need me to do?"

As he rushed by the open fire, he thrust the pieces of metal into the coals then ducked down behind the forge. "Keep watch and come up with a good cover story. If someone sneaks up on us, I'm not going to be able to just grab the pieces of the sword and run."

She couldn't imagine that they'd have more than a couple of hours even if they were lucky. "How long is this going to take?"

He looked nervously around the edge of town. "I'm just going to do a forge weld. It won't be nearly as strong or pretty as the original, but it should work for decapitations. If Marjory's body is being watched by some fairy-tale royal guard, one measly sword isn't going to do us much good anyway."

"Personally, from what we're seeing in these dimensions, I'm hoping for the seven dwarfs."

He snickered as he gathered up the tools he'd need from the bench, staying low enough not to be seen by anyone hiding in a house. "I don't think anyone is going to believe her as Snow White. Sleeping Beauty, cursed to slumber a hundred years, would fit better with Marjory's age."

"If we ever have to enter this building again, I'll need to brush up on my folklore."

SERE BREATHED a little easier back out in the stairwell.

"What the hell is this?" Doodlebug yanked the sword from Bart's grasp.

"It's the best I could do on short notice and with

seventeenth-century equipment." His even tone told Sere he hadn't taken the criticism well.

Doodlebug tried to swing the mangled blade through the air. "It looks like something for killing orcs."

Bart snatched the sword back from the girl. "Let's hope that's not what we'll be facing. Do you know anything about where Marjory stashed her body?"

"It's only two floors below us." The girl turned back toward the stairs and began to climb down.

"I meant, something I don't already know."

Even from half a floor behind, Sere caught the girl's shrug of indifference. "I only entered the two floors you were just on and the restaurant on top of the tower," Doodlebug said.

At the door marked *Floor Seventeen*, Sere felt her heart pounding, but this time, it wasn't from the stairs. "Are we sure we're not doing exactly what Marjory wants? Once she's back in human form, she might have yet another trick up her sleeve that we haven't anticipated."

Bart leaned against the wall. "We haven't even gotten the body back yet. When we force her spirit back into it, we'll have Joe's security guards on our side. Even though she may have hired them, I heard the resolute tone of acceptance when their leader talked to you. They'll be on our side even if she does come back to life."

Doodlebug kicked the door repeatedly as if riling up a nest of hornets. "They're still small potatoes compared to the head loa of the dead. How well do you trust Baron Samedi? Seems like he's playing referee in this little magical contest."

"At this point, I'm not even sure if his input matters. He's going to do whatever he wants. I'm just trying to anticipate Marjory's next move." Sere looked at Bart, hoping his military-trained mind had come up with a logical next step.

He stared at the girl kicking the door until she got the message. "Marjory's soul is still on the sidelines, and we've got an unexpected advantage. She wanted to keep her body safe, so she wouldn't have just stashed it anywhere in time. She would have chosen a situation where a comatose woman would be under guard. I hate to say it, but the story of Sleeping Beauty—or at least the events that inspired the story—might be exactly what's behind that door."

"Great." Though unable to lie, Doodlebug had developed a uniquely annoying form of sarcasm. "Anyone remember the fairy tale? Because I'm going to tell you, Dooly didn't spend much time being read to as a child."

Bart shook his head as if the story was in there somewhere and he was trying to dislodge it from his mental bookshelf. "Other than her being cursed to sleep for a hundred years in a castle and woken up by a handsome prince, I've got nothing."

Sere sat on the metal stair. Memories of her previous life were ethereal and based more on emotions than facts. "The Grimm brothers' fairy tales were all the rage when I was a little girl. My mother used to read them to me in the original German. I remember the stories even though I haven't got a clue how to speak the language."

"Is this really helping?" Doodlebug stuck close to the door as if there were some danger lurking in the stairwell.

Sere attempted to be more specific. "After the princess

falls asleep, she's laid out on the finest bed in the castle. The rest of the living people and animals are also put to sleep so they'll be with her when she awakes."

"That's good news," Bart said. "They can't fight us if they're sleeping."

"She said *living* people." Doodlebug ran her hand over the lever. "That doesn't do us any good if Marjory had her doppelgänger send in a security detail from hell."

Sere was still trying to separate out the details of the story from all the rest of the books she'd heard as a child. "Doodlebug is right. The story talked of trees and bramble overgrowing the walls to keep the princess safe. There's something about snakes too, but that's about all I can remember."

Bart held the sword up like a medieval knight. "This should work against branches and vines. Time we got to work."

"So, who's playing doorman this time?" Doodlebug kept hold of the handle.

Sere could only see one option. "Bart's best with the sword, and I know my way around weird dimensions. Since Marjory used my body to sneak hers onto this floor, maybe I'll have some ability to work around her safety features. That means you'll stand guard."

Doodlebug crossed her arms and leaned against the door. "I'm getting really tired of playing the servant around you."

Sere didn't have time for the girl's theatrics. "When this is over, we'll figure out a better division of labor, but for right now, Bart and I have to retrieve Marjory."

"I don't like it." Doodlebug turned back to the latch.

"Wait." Bart grabbed the girl's wrist. "You opened the doors the last two times, and both times, we ended up where you landed in those dimensions."

"So?" Doodlebug didn't take her hand from the door.

"If we enter this realm where you would start, we'd probably be somewhere out in the forest, where we'd have to fight our way in. If we go in the way Sere-Marjory did, maybe we can bypass the bramble and start out closer to the sleeping body."

"Or maybe Marjory is smarter than you two, and you both will end up back in the vault. Did you even think of that? The mercenary downstairs already proved Sere's handprint no longer matches what it was like the last time her body entered the building."

Sere pushed Doodlebug aside. "No, it matched Joe's hand, and he was well known by the people who ran this institution. Marjory might have anticipated me coming back to the World Trade Center, but there's no way she could have imagined Joe coming back to life." She grabbed the handle and pushed it down.

SERE STOOD next to Bart in the round room with stairs circling up to the second floor from either side. "That girl is getting too big for her britches."

"You weren't much better when we first met. I assume we have to go upstairs." He held the sword at the ready as he scanned the room. Dressed in a long white tunic that covered his chain mail, the big man with the sword would have fit right in with any knight contingent.

"I'm surprised there isn't a welcoming party. Doesn't seem like Marjory to bait the trap with her body then wait to spring it until we were within striking distance." Sere reached for her boot but ended up with a handful of chiffon. "I wish I had my knife."

Bart took a little longer looking her over than was prudent considering the unseen dangers. "Though I would have preferred to find you in some leather disguise as the woodland thief, I've gotta say, you make a stunning princess."

"Thanks for not calling me a damsel in distress." She led the way to the staircase.

"I don't think anyone will ever make that mistake." The interlinking rings of metal rattled as he walked.

As she put her foot on the first white marble tread, a dragon emerged upstairs, filling the hallway. "I think we found our combatant. Looks like Marjory refined her dragon-summoning charm."

The dragon's claw curled over the stair at the top of the arc. "You're not welcome here." His raspy voice reminded her so much of how she'd sounded to herself when using Smoke's reptilian vocal cords that she put her hand to her throat.

Bart brushed past Sere. With only the mangled sword, he wasn't going to be a match for the fire breather. "I suspect you're also an intruder in this magical realm. I wonder how the powers that run this place will feel about monsters invading their territory."

Flames erupted from the beast's nose and mouth, setting the elegant banister ablaze and scorching the stone. The dragon crept down toward the crouching knight.

"He's coming down at you." From the bottom of the staircase, Sere had a better view of the action than her champion. She felt beyond helpless.

Bart sprang so far up the stairs that she wondered if there was another knight she hadn't noticed. With one powerful swing of the sword, he cut a bloody line across the dragon's throat. He then used the momentum to get clear of the beast's teeth and claws. Though successful in landing the cutting edge to flesh, all he'd really accomplished was proving that the sword was no match for a dragon of that size.

Shit. Now what do we do?

The stained-glass window that cast shades of red, yellow, and purple onto the staircase seemed to come to life as the shading shifted to shadows. Glass exploded across the entire circular great room. Flames covered the ceiling.

"Back off, Flambeaux."

Sere nearly darted up the stairs when she recognized Smoke's voice, but the smaller dragon that had confronted Bart wasn't the cowardly type she'd previously encountered from Marjory's creations.

"I was hoping you'd show, *Bernie*."

"Har, har." The big dragon's attempt at a fake laugh melted what little was left of the glass as he stood on the window's stone ledge. "Now, are you going to come out here and fight me, or are you going to hide in your snake hole?"

The castle dragon backed up to the top of the stairs. As he turned toward Smoke, Sere saw an opportunity for Bart to run his sword into the spread scales. But to her surprise, he remained close to the wall as the flying serpent pursued the larger dragon out the window.

"Now's our chance." His whisper was barely louder than the flapping wings outside.

She rushed up to him. "Why didn't you skewer the dragon?"

"He would have turned back to us. Couldn't you tell that Smoke was running a distraction play? So long as Flambeaux is outside, we're clear to grab Marjory."

Though what he said made sense, she still wanted to see the monster coughing blood with his flames. "There must be something about this dimension that's riling up my demon side."

"Probably the same thing that made Flambeaux chase Smoke. My guess would be that it has something to do with the door sensor thinking you were human. A heightened connection to hell didn't seem to be a problem on the other two floors."

Bart found the strangest times to analyze events. Sere considered arguing that Smoke either had something to do with the change or had made it across because of it, but either way, the discussion would simply be wasting time. "We'd better get moving."

He took off down the hallway that had housed Flambeaux. Without checking the line of rooms, he headed straight to the massive double doors at the end and busted through them.

The body of Marjory Laroque lay on a bed covered by a white-silk comforter edged in gold. Her gown so perfectly matched the covering that her figure could have been mistaken for ripples and folds in the bedspread. Bart handed Sere the sword. "I can carry her or defend our escape, but I can't do both."

She took the sword, feeling instantly more like her old self. "One task done. Now we just have to get down to the building's lobby."

He threw Marjory over his shoulder and raced back down the hallway. In her overly fluffy gown, Sere struggled to keep up. As he reached the stairs, she was still half a hallway behind—just far enough to see Flambeaux cruise through the shattered window. Flames followed the monster, announcing that Smoke wasn't far behind.

She hitched up her skirts with one hand and pumped all her energy into her legs. Marjory's dragon was just bending his neck down the stairs when she aimed the blade straight at it. The crudely repaired sword's welded and sharpened shards of metal separated the reptile's protective scales. Blood spewed onto Sere as the huge beast succumbed to the direct blow. He tumbled over the charred railing. His crash onto the marble-inlay floor rumbled the castle.

Though she needed to hustle after Bart, Sere turned back to Smoke. "Thanks, but how are you here?"

He nodded at the sword. "When that thing encountered the foreign dimension of Salem, Chloe got word from the World Trade Center's custodian. We figured this would be where you needed me. Since I was created to watch over

Doodlebug, with her holding the door open—even from your dimension—I was able to slip through."

She shook her head. "I'm sorry I asked. Thanks again. Every warrior from hell should have a trusty dragon."

WITH THE MILITIA that had served Joe so well guarding every door and window in the lobby, Sere watched with sword in hand as Bart tipped the blue-glass jar to the mouth of the comatose Marjory Laroque. With Gerald holding the woman's nose, the body had no choice but to swallow the liquid.

The revived Marjory rolled onto her stomach, coughing and choking so badly that Sere wondered if the potion would do the job of killing the woman and save her the trouble. Unfortunately, Marjory struggled to her feet, forcing her body to behave. As Bart, Doodlebug, Gerald, and Aloysius stood near the guards, Marjory focused on Sere and the blood-dripping sword.

"So, you're just going to execute me in cold blood? Sounds like something the devil's daughter would do." The woman's sneer sounded more demonic than human.

Still covered in dragon blood, Sere wondered if the woman was right. Maybe she was giving in to her demonic side. But Kendell's solution of building hell and consigning Baron Malveaux to that prison hadn't worked out so well either. "My father, your ancestor, took over the body of your son, Lincoln. If Kendell and her gang had acted as judge, jury, and executioner right then and there, none of this nightmare would have happened. He wouldn't have been able to reach back in time and steal my soul. I would have passed through Guinee and ended up in eternal rest. Father's soul would have been turned over to the loas of the dead. Hell wouldn't even have existed. Doppelgängers, demons, and devils would only be the topics of folklore."

"So by killing me, you right the wrongs of those who saved you? Hell will still exist when I'm dead. That idiot loa might have isolated our dear departed from the *deep waters*, but he can't go around scooping up our whole family. Kill me, and I'll just return in another form."

"And I'll be here to greet you when you do." Sere had grown tired of arguments that only served to let evil squirm away. Without thinking, she let her eyesight go red and swung the sword with all of the combined strength of those who supported her. Marjory's head flew halfway across the room and landed at her brother's feet.

WHILE MARJORY'S body continued oozing blood onto the marble floor at Sere's feet—mixing with the dragon blood that dripped from her sword and clothing—Sere turned to Aloysius. "Now, what are we going to do about you?"

Gerald stepped into the gore. "We had an arrangement. I stood aside while you did what you had to do with my sister, but I will not let you cut down my grandson in cold blood."

She glanced down at her body and sword. His assumption that she was out to kill Aloysius did make a certain amount of visual sense. "I didn't mean to imply that I intended to kill him. Baron Samedi will take Marjory's soul as his answer to the other loas, but he has made it clear that only one immortal can remain among the living, and we haven't got a clue as to how to separate Aloysius back into his component parts."

Aloysius placed his hand on his grandfather's arm, and the old man quietly relinquished center stage. "I know what I have to do. I've been giving this some thought since we met with Baron Samedi. With Great-Aunt Marjory gone, there's really only one option for me. I have to go to hell. Her doppelgänger will dissipate soon enough, leaving a void in the balance of power. We can't just hand the reins over to the Cormorant and let her rule the underworld."

"You would become the devil?" Gerald asked, his near whisper echoing around the glass-and-steel room.

Aloysius stood a little straighter as if the hesitant man was turning into a commanding authority before Sere's eyes. "No. Hell's ruler doesn't have to be a devil. Instead of using our shared ancestor as my model the way Marjory did, I would follow your lead, Grandfather. You didn't demand loyalty of your force—you inspired it. Instead of coerced obedience, you laid out a system of justice for this city's citizens, great and small." He turned toward Doodlebug. "Part of me was there when the Doppel Avenger stood up for the suffering doppelgängers. You had a team of warriors. Your example proves the realm doesn't have to be a constant torture."

Doodlebug took Aloysius's hand. "I'll do what I can from this side, but you can't ask me to return. Though that might be your destiny, even the devil's daughter hasn't asked that much of me."

His head dropped. "Give me your contacts. Tell me how to win them over. I know I can make that world a place worth living in."

Sere feared she might still be replacing one devil with another. "You'll be cut off from this reality. You and I will live eternity on the seesaw that straddles hell and life."

When he lifted his head, she could have sworn she was looking in the eyes of a new ruler. "I won't invade your domain if you promise to never again set foot in hell. That will be our accord."

"And the Cormorant?" Though she could no longer feel a connection to the birdwoman, Sere knew that turning her back on the mirror of Jennifer in hell was overly risky. "Your great-aunt's dragons have been burned to a crisp like deep-fried chicken. Her play to win over the general doppelgänger population with promises of freedom from the harvesters has failed. The Cormorant will mark for dismemberment anyone who is carrying one of her precious coins. She holds all the cards."

"Not quite." Doodlebug patted the toe of her army boot in the red pool, mixing the darker shade of dragon blood with that of its mistress.

Aloysius gave a familial smile of dominance—one that Sere had encountered throughout her strange existence. She could only hope it didn't always foretell evil intentions.

"Being the underdog has advantages," he said. "The Cormorant will think she's won, but if I have the Doppel Avenger's army and come in riding on the dragon that slew

Madam Laroque's squadrons, that will give the average doppelgänger a hero to look to for salvation. Tell me you wouldn't take those odds."

Sere took hold of the blood-soaked blade and aimed the handle at Aloysius. "I won't call you a king. You'll need to come up with your own title, but a ruler should have a sword."

Aloysius grasped the handle of the mythical Excalibur.

Bart leaned in toward Sere. "If you give him that one, what are we going to do about Arthur?"

Sere had already contemplated his question. "I can't have the Lady of the Lake hand the king of the Britons that mangled hunk of steel anyway. Call Dooly Buell. She should still have the matching katana that we used to train the girls. He'll never know the difference. If there really is magic imbedded in objects, that sword in Aloysius's hand belongs in hell."

22

*S*ere stretched out on the bed as the last rays of daylight filtered in through the dormer window that faced Frenchmen Street. "Do we have to go?"

Bart lay on his back completely naked, his magnificent sweaty body gleaming in the light. "We've been fucking, showering, eating, and fucking some more all day. By now, you must be ready to see other people. Besides, you are kind of the guest of honor."

Two floors below, the band was ramping up loudly enough that it could be heard through the open back window that looked down on the courtyard. She curled back over his luscious body, arching her thigh upward to tease the base of his cock back into a building erection. "Not as much as I want to keep you all to myself."

His hand, which had been caressing her side, came to an abrupt stop. "What's that sound?"

Shit. Now what? She tuned out the sound of the band and

heard the distinctive gentle humming of the old Triumph engine. "That's my Triton." She bounced out of bed and ran for the door.

"Put something on first." Bart threw a pair of jeans and a halter top at her from the clothing scattered about the floor.

Like performing a fighting tumble, she had the items on right before she slammed through the door. She slid down the banister and was outside the building as the beloved engine shut down. "What are you doing with my motorcycle?" She hadn't meant to yell.

Doodlebug pulled off the full-face helmet. "Someone said you were looking for it." She leaned to the side to display her passenger.

In jeans, leather boots, and Sere's skullcap helmet, Jennifer could have finally passed for Sere's twin. "We found it in an abandoned garage in the Tremé. A very nice homeless dude explained he was keeping an eye on it. I think he thought I was you." When she swung her leg off the back seat, Sere noticed the two snakes wrapped around her neck like a scarf.

Sere stood with her fists against the side belt loops of her jeans. "What's with you two traitors?"

The serpents unwound from Jennifer's neck and hissed their greetings at Sere. They fell to the ground and wiggled toward her like puppies who'd been too long away from their mama.

"They bared their fangs at me when we finally pried open the plywood door to the garage. Apparently, they knew the difference between us. At first, they remained coiled on the seat like they weren't going to let me get anywhere near the motorcycle, but once I started talking to them, they warmed up to me. You know, Bobby would lose his mind if he saw me with two snakes coiled around my neck."

Sere nodded toward the Triton. "At least you weren't foolhardy enough to try to drive it yourself."

Jennifer led the way to the door of the Scratchy Dog. "And cross you? I wouldn't think of it. But I am going to hold you to giving me riding lessons. Sitting behind Doodlebug for the short ride here was a blast."

Bart slipped his arm around Sere's waist. "Nobody dead?"

She nudged him with her elbow. "Not this time, wiseass. Without Marjory around to summon new demons and with the hellmouth as closed as it can be, I guess I'm going to have to learn new ways of interacting with people."

Jennifer looked over her shoulder as she entered the club. "We'll be here to help."

As Sere stepped into the familiar bar, she did her usual visual sweep of the room. This time, however, she wasn't making a quick assessment of tactical advantages and potential threats. Instead, she let her attention drift to each person who'd been such an important part of her life.

With Polly and Kendell as his dance partners, Fisher worked his moves in front of the stage. Sere could just imagine the man in his younger years trying to attract the attention of the members of Polly Urethane and the Strippers. Now he was dancing with them.

She caught the feminine laughter of Fisher's wife and daughters as they hung out at the bar and watched the older, more conservative husband and father. Myles fixed the women drinks while regaling them with stories of the man's superhero-sidekick adventures. With any luck, they'd only believe half of the yarns Myles was spinning.

Professor Yates sat alone at a corner table, smoking his pipe. At least the consummate observer had finally left his lab. "Considering how paranoid he's gotten after all of this time working with doppelgängers, I'm surprised Polly got him out of his security blanket."

Bart noticed where she was looking. "We invited Gerald Laroque, thinking the two elderly gentlemen might find some common ground, but he respectfully declined."

Sere wasn't surprised the former chief of police had chosen not to attend. "Even though every person here knows he's an ally, he likes helping from the shadows. I suspect *not* being here is his way of telling us he's still on guard in case we need him."

Sere's guard went up when she noticed Doodlebug approach Dooly Buell at the far end of the bar. With both of them living in the same city, some interaction was inevitable. "We're going to have to watch that pair."

Bart's hand hadn't left her back. "While you were out saving the world, the rest of us had a talk with Dooly. We've set her up with some educators the professor knows. She'll be attending Delgado Community College's continuing education program to get her GED. From there, and with all of our tutelage, hopefully, she'll continue on toward higher education."

Sere leaned against his side and smiled. "I like that. How did she react to the opportunity?"

"She was hesitant at first, but working with Polly on the professor's computer simulation has sparked a curiosity we hope can be fanned into something more meaningful."

Sere couldn't imagine Doodlebug following the same course for her life, but then, it was hard to say what interests would filter through their connection. She was so focused on the people she cared about that she didn't notice Chloe until the swamp witch twirled her diaphanous green dress in front of her. "Isn't that music just divine? I couldn't resist dancing in the moonlight, but when I saw you come in, I forced myself to join the party."

Bernie made a beeline for the two at the end of the bar and ordered an absinth for Chloe. Though neither Dooly nor Doodlebug embraced the handsome young man, Sere felt they both wanted to. They covered their latent desire with sarcastic comments about him being Chloe's errand boy.

The swamp witch continued her ethereal dance moves as she swung in front of Sere with Bart and Jennifer still at her sides. "I have a surprise for you," Chloe said.

Sere never had the best luck when it came to people's surprises. "What have you done now?"

"Look behind you."

Sere swung around so fast that Bart's hand, which had been around her back, now acted as a restraint around her waist.

"Hi, Sere." Sanguine no longer had either her wings or her magically faceted eyes, but not all angel attributes were meant to be seen.

Sere busted through Bart's embrace and threw her arms

around Sanguine's neck. When she knew the woman wasn't merely a projection from another realm, she squeezed tighter. "How are you here?"

Sanguine's grip around her waist reminded Sere of being lifted into the air on the woman's wings. "We need to have a talk about that, but let me say hi to Kendell and the others first. It's been a long time since we've been in the same dimension."

Even if Sere had pressed for an immediate answer, it wouldn't have mattered. Kendell ran so fast across the dance floor that Sere let go of Sanguine to search for the incoming disaster. The women slammed together into a hug that quieted the room. "I missed you so much." Kendell's words were muffled behind Sanguine's long white hair.

DOODLEBUG REMAINED hunched over her beer as the rest of the room swirled around the two women. She had to time her approach with care. If she moved too soon, she'd be spotted, but if she waited too long, the old fart would get up from his chair. When Dooly followed Bernie away from the counter, she saw her chance. After getting up, she circled behind the people facing away from the front door. With the place locked up for the private affair, she didn't have to worry about random people pushing their way in. Professor Yates was just sliding his chair out from the table when she pulled Bart's knife from the center of her belt. With one quick lunge, she had the sharp edge against his throat.

"What the hell do you think you're doing?"

Though she'd accounted for everyone, Bernie had an annoying habit of keeping an eye on her. Apparently, Dooly hadn't been the distraction she'd hoped for. The idiot's voice of alarm attracted the attention of the emotional fools huddled in the center of the room.

"He has to pay. He created hell, then he stood by as evil took hold. Everything that's happened has been his fault. I promised Aloysius I would help remake hell, and this is the first step." Her hand holding the blade wavered against his throat.

Professor Yates held his pipe out to his side as if he thought he was going to get another drag of the tobacco. "I did create hell. I won't argue with you on that point."

"He's not the devil." Polly stood in front of the pack like a protective she-wolf. "You and Sere just went to considerable lengths to take care of the last one. Think about what you're doing, Doodlebug. We've all had a hand in creating you and the realm you protected."

She held the knife with resolve. "No. He's the one most responsible for hell, and that makes him worse than the devil. He's the god behind the creation. Whether he likes it or not, he created hell and everyone in it, yet he just sat back in his chair and watched it play out. Where was he when my doppelgänger brothers and sisters turned into harvesters? Why did he mirror evil people? He could have chosen only those who cared about others. Why didn't his damn program favor those who wanted to help instead of leaving everything to chance? Why did *I* have to become the Doppel Avenger? None of this had to happen if he'd only shown a little preference toward those out to do some good. God has to pay for his sins."

"Put the knife down." Sere moved up next to Polly with her own blade in hand. "He's helped more than you'll ever know."

"Not me, he hasn't." Doodlebug gritted her teeth to combat the emotions that hit her from Dooly like waves off the ocean. "This old fool never once answered my pleas for help. He just sat in his lab, watching hell on his little diorama like it was a soap opera. We're real beings—maybe not human, but we've got lives that deserve respect. What did he think was going to happen when he abandoned us in hell?"

Polly kept her hands out as if she thought Doodlebug would consider her any kind of a threat. "There's a better way."

Doodlebug pressed the blade against his flabby flesh. "There is no other way. He has to be held responsible."

"Listen to me for just a moment," Polly said. "You're right about us not getting involved when we should have. We were missing a fundamental part of the equation—the doppelgänger perspective. We didn't have you. If you're serious about changing hell, killing Cornelius isn't going to accomplish that. Join us. Let me teach you how the program works. Together, we can make that realm a better place. Doesn't that work better than alienating yourself from the inner workings?"

Doodlebug eased off of her pressure against the old man's throat. "You're just trying to trick me. I've seen the way people lie."

"They're not." Dooly stepped out from behind the throng of people. "We both know I'm not smart enough to understand what Polly has been trying to teach me. That's why they're paying for me to go back to school—everything from food and lodging to tuition and textbooks. Being across the river will prevent us from being together and causing a problem with the equipment, and it will allow me to funnel the improved mental skills through to you. We can do this, Doodlebug, you and me. If you're serious about wanting to change hell, this is the way to do it. If you just want to give in to your anger against your god, then none of us can stop you."

Doodlebug's eyes filled with tears, and much as she hated to admit it, they weren't from Dooly's emotions. She lowered the weapon. "Don't expect me to ask for forgiveness."

Professor Yates took a shaky long drag from his pipe. "You've made a very strong argument for me being more involved in my creation. I expect it will be both a pleasure and a challenge working with you."

Before Doodlebug could realize he was behind her, Bart took the knife from her hand. "We're all in this together."

Sanguine took Sere's hand. "It's time we had that talk. The professor isn't the only one in the room with something to atone for."

Sere was still shaking with anger at Doodlebug and frustration with herself for not seeing the danger. She didn't want to turn her back on the doppelbitch again. After the girl had killed Joe, Sere never should have let her near any of her friends. But at least with Doodlebug showing her true colors, everyone would be forever on guard around her.

"The courtyard out back is empty." Sere grabbed a bottle of Jameson and two glasses before leading the way down the side hallway.

Outside in the moonlight, Sanguine pulled Sere's cell phone from her jeans and they took their seats on the metal chairs. "Try not to lose this again." Free from the large wings, the woman leaned back as if finally able to correctly stretch out. "I forgot how peaceful the nights can be here."

"I didn't think you'd ever leave hell." Sere couldn't stop staring at Sanguine. She felt like a child seeing her parent as a normal adult for the first time.

Sanguine poured a sizable amount of whiskey into her glass and downed it in one shot. "The demon outbreak was my fault. I'm the reason the hellmouth has stayed open for all this time. I'm the rift."

Sere never understood the human need to play the martyr. "Don't be ridiculous. You spent twenty years as hell's angel, raising the devil's daughter. If anyone's to blame, it's me. The doppelgängers achieved consciousness due to my actions. I was the first one out of the gate. They simply followed my example."

Sanguine added more alcohol to both of their glasses. "I know you think it's that simple, but you're wrong. I've been a fool—not that I would have changed that much. Raising you was my life's mission. *That* wasn't the problem. My arrogance was in thinking I could save you from hell's influences once you'd grown up. Every problem you've had to face since you were let out of hell has arisen because of my stupidity."

Sere could tell that the self-condemnation Sanguine was expressing was sincere. "I don't understand."

"Agnes built the hellmouth so she could transport her creations to the other dimension. So long as she was on that side, the door remained open so she could return. Like her, I'm human, so the gate functioned the same way while I was in hell. The problem started when I borrowed some of my grandmother's magic to sprout wings and grow eyes that could see the future. Living in hell while making my body into a hybrid between the two dimensions ripped at the seam that separated the two realities. I thought if you and I hid out in the swamp while you grew up, I could keep others from rushing through the hellmouth and I could contain the rip. When I cleared the way for you to leave, the love I hold for you increased the rift. The only answer was for me to return to this dimension where I belong."

Sere swallowed half of her drink. "So now the hellmouth is closed for good?"

"I believe so."

Sere couldn't imagine living her life without constantly looking over her shoulder for some demon or devil on the rise. "I only had a few months to taste life before Monty made his appearance. It's been pretty much a nonstop whirlwind of terror ever since." She looked at the woman, seeking out the angel who'd always protected her. "What am I supposed to do now?"

Sanguine stared into her drink. "If you want my advice, go marry Rampart Thibodaux. Not next year, or next month, or even next week—go do it tonight. Stop wasting time. Allow yourself to be vulnerable. Make a fool of yourself. Go ask him in front of everyone who cares about you. In your heart you know he'll say yes. Stop hiding behind your intellect."

"And what do I do as he ages?" The conflict between her immortality and his eventual death was one that had been plaguing Sere since their first time together.

Sanguine looked into Sere's eyes. The woman's magical sight might have left her, but the wisdom of seeing multiple paths remained in the sapphire pools of light. "Follow Jennifer's lead, and age with him. Grow old, Sere. Enjoy every stage of life right up to and including Bart's ultimate death. Don't waste a minute of it."

"And then what?" If Sanguine intended on pulling at Sere's threads of self-doubt, she was going to have to face all of her deepest, darkest questions.

"Revert to your younger self and do it all over again. Find someone else to love, but don't make the same mistakes you made this time through life. Tell them you love them sooner. Don't play the foolish games that keep you apart. You have the gift of getting to discover what most of us can only guess at."

Sere stared at the one-time angel, trying to figure out what she would have done in Sanguine's place. "You looked into the future, didn't you?"

She reached out and took Sere's hands. "Only to see your professional path. Hell isn't going away, and that means you're still needed. The professor's time is nearly finished, but for the most part, Polly has already taken over his duties. When it comes to the paranormal science that maintains the doppelgängers, hell will be in good hands. When Polly's time is over, Doodlebug will take over from her. Hell will finally be in the care of a doppelgänger who understands the true dynamics of what it means to live in that dimension. However, Doodlebug will need your guidance to get there."

"And the other two legs of hell?"

Sanguine's smile carried wisdom beyond her fortysomething years. "I've already turned over the Wiccan reins to Chloe Aberrant. She's training Bernie, who will take over when her time is up. You know the swamp as well as anyone. Watching over the succession of swamp witches will be your responsibility, but you won't have to worry about that for some time. Bernie will help you find the right person when his time is up, but never forget the swamp is your home. Don't lose control of it."

"Speaking of control, I can't deal with Baron Samedi directly. Voodoo isn't something I can command."

"You won't have to." Sanguine leaned in close as if there was someone else in the courtyard who might be listening in. "They don't know it yet, but Kendell and Myles are going to have a son."

"Isn't she a little old?" Sere nearly laughed at her own ageism.

"Women in their forties can still bear children, especially when the small human soul has a loa of the dead as his godfather." Sanguine's expression lost some of its excitement. "You're going to have to keep an eye on that one."

Sere was pretty sure she didn't want to know what Sanguine had seen. "So, I sit back and watch everyone I know die while worrying that hell will find a way to once again invade the living?"

"Listen to me. You are the most precious being I've ever known. You are my daughter in every way but biological. Bart loves you with a fierce passion that would take on the living or the damned. Jennifer sees you as a twin sister—the adventurous one she always wanted to be. To Kendell and Myles, you're their validation for saving the world from Baron Malveaux. Fisher, Professor Yates, Polly, and everyone else who've put their lives and souls on the line for you have found it an honor to join in your fight for good over evil."

Sere had never found compliments or shows of affection comfortable. "Stop blowing smoke up my ass. You're not answering my question."

Sanguine shook her head. "You don't get it, do you? You're no longer hooked to hell. As a doppelgänger, you don't need the basics of life, but the power that sustains you no longer comes from that foreign dimension."

Sere felt as dense as the bricks that surrounded her. "I don't understand. What are you telling me?"

"*Love*, Sere. That's what keeps you alive. That's your purpose. That's what powers you, body and soul. If you ever choose to let go of your immortality, all you have to do is cut yourself off from those who care about you. With no psychic connections, you will truly age. So when I say embrace your love of Bart, that's only the beginning. Fuck what the professor said. Get to know Jennifer. Become Bobby's favorite aunt. When the time is right, tell him your secrets. When Bart does pass on to the *deep waters*, you'll need someone who knows all about you but isn't involved in watching over hell. Bobby can help ease you into a new life. I can only see your life to the next curve in this reality's path, but that path is made up of people you love and who love you. You're no longer the devil's daughter. You belong in this life. That's your mission now."

Sere couldn't figure out why tears were filling her eyes. "And what about you?"

Sanguine leaned back and looked at the night sky. "I've spent so much time looking into possible futures that it will be interesting to live in the moment. I'm no longer hell's angel, but I'm also not sure I fit in this life. The swamp beckons me home. I intend on living out my days with the plants and animals, though without seeing the future, I don't know where my life will lead me. Lefty swam me through the gate and is waiting for me back on Agnes's island. Out there, I'll be close to the hellmouth. Our friendly gator will forever act as hell's watchdog in case there's another outbreak. So if you ever need help, you know exactly where to find him."

BOOK LIST

Technopia Series:
(writing as Greg Chase)
Creation
Evolution
Damnation
Salvation

The Malveaux Curse Mysteries :
(writing as G.A. Chase)
Dog Days of Voodoo
You, Me, and the Voodoo Queen
Oops! I Voodooed Again
Voodoo You Love
Voodoo You Think You Are
Look What You Made Me Voodoo
Love Me Like Voodoo

The Devil's Daughter:
(writing as G.A. Chase)
Hell in a Head Gasket
Hell Bent for Demons

Hell's Highway
Hell or High Water
Hell Away from Home
Hell and Back

ABOUT THE AUTHOR

G.A. Chase is the pen name for Greg Chase. He is a science fiction and paranormal author living in New Orleans with his wife, fellow author Deanna Chase, and their two shih tzu dogs. On any given day you can find him behind his computer, people watching in the Quarter, or out in his studio creating stories in glass. His glass work can be found at www.chase-designs.com.

gregchaseauthor.com

www.ingramcontent.com/pod-product-compliance
Lightning Source LLC
Chambersburg PA
CBHW020310200626
46814CB00006BA/2175